LOST BOYS

LOST BOYS

stories by

DARCI BYSOUTH

thistledown press

Thistledown Press Ltd.
410 2nd Avenue North
Saskatoon, Saskatchewan, S7K 2C3
www.thistledownpress.com

Library and Archives Canada Cataloguing in Publication
Title: Lost boys / stories by Darci Bysouth.
Names: Bysouth, Darci, 1968- author.
Identifiers: Canadiana (print) 20190134593 | Canadiana (ebook)
20190134607 | ISBN 9781771871754
(softcover) | ISBN 9781771871761 (HTML) | ISBN 9781771871778
(PDF)
Classification: LCC PS8603.Y86 L68 2019 | DDC C813/.6—dc23

Cover: photograph from **Cueva de las Manos (Cave of Hands)**,
Santa Cruz, Argentina, circa 7300 BC
Cover and book design by Jackie Forrie
Printed and bound in Canada
Author photo by Peter Kalasz

Canada

Canada Council
for the Arts
Conseil des Arts
du Canada

Thistledown Press gratefully acknowledges the financial assistance of
the Canada Council for the Arts, the Saskatchewan Arts Board, and the
Government of Canada for its publishing program.

Acknowledgements

The author would like to thank the editors of the following magazines and periodicals for publishing earlier versions of some of these stories: *The Antigonish Review* (Issue 92), Appletree Writer's *In on the Shore, The Bridport Anthology 2012, New Writing Scotland* (Issue 30), *Cutthroat: A Journal of the Arts* (Volume 12 Issue 1), Bridge House's *On This Day*, and *The Bristol Prize Anthology* (Volume 3).

Thanks to my teachers at the University of Edinburgh: Douglas Dougan for showing me how to see the story, Gavin Inglis for insisting I choose the right words, and George Anderson for making me look the audience in the eye. My gratitude to the very much missed Helen Lamb, whose mentorship fostered myself and so many others.

Thanks to the folks at Thistledown Press, and particularly to John Lent, for his kindness, patience and keen insight in editing these stories.

Thanks to my family for providing a peaceful place in which to create. And finally, my gratitude to Brian and Deanna, for their unflagging encouragement and enthusiasm.

To my Muse, the original lost boy

Contents

All Things Come To Pass

The Night Passing Through

Weighting Down the Dark

ALL THINGS COME TO PASS

BETWEEN SEA AND SHORE

I HAVE TO CROSS THE WATER to find him. One ocean was behind me, flown over in a haze of engine roar and low oxygen, the hours passed in meal trays and movies while I looked for breaks in the cloud cover. The water was such a long way below that it looked like some other thing; static, dead as stone. That night in my hotel room I dreamed of slipping into those waves and the water setting like concrete in my mouth, and when my alarm woke me I could not move. But there is still a sea crossing to come, and this is the trickier one.

I make the long drive north through the grey towns and churning turbines, past the scrambling sheep and occasional cow, and north still, to where the rock crumbles to sand. The barrenness surprises me; I'd expected lush hills or rolling heather. Then I turn a bend and the sea swings into view. It's a warm tropical teal, and edged with pure white sand. A cloud passes and the sky darkens, and the sea is once again that sullen navy. Transient, illusory. It occurs to me that I really could find him here. My belly clenches.

The ferryman is waiting on the dock, smoking a cigarette.

"Cannae take your car," he says, "You come by foot or not at all."

So I pocket my keys and hand over my silver. My ribs press against the rusted railings while I wait. There's a damp fog coming in that's deadening sight and sound, and leaving me neither here nor there. The ferryman flicks his ash to sea and turns, gesturing for me to come.

I could go back. I could tell Dylan he wasn't there and I could watch Dylan pretend detachment: "Yeah cool, mom, I've done without him all my life so what's the difference?"

But the ferryman waits and I've already paid. I hoist my suitcase up the gangplank.

This sea is nothing like stone. It twists and chops, and the small boat heaves. I lean over the railings to retch and the ferryman looks the other way. I'm thankful for the fog, for the way it throws a curtain between us, and for the fact that I am the only passenger.

The mist has lifted by the time we reach the village. The little white boats bob in the harbour with their masts jutting like needles from a satin sea, and the houses glow crayon-bright in a setting sun. It's familiar from the BBC children's programme Dylan and I would watch when he was little. The opening credits would pan over the smooth sea and untroubled sky, through the open doors of those bright houses and onto the smiling faces, and into a world where every upset could be remedied with enough twinkly application. Dylan could do the rolling accents perfectly and this spooked me; I wasn't sure if it was a new-found talent or some kind of genetic memory. He asked for the video when he was sick, or when he twisted restless and would not soothe. It calmed him, this place where the worst that could go missing was a letter or key, where all lost things would be recovered before tea-time. But Dylan turned sixteen last spring.

"You never looked for him. You never told me his name," he said, glaring at his computer screen. "You never even told him, did you? About me." His knee juddered underneath the table.

At sixteen, you don't know the sea change a few words can bring.

My son stared at me and rocked back in his chair, his eyes dark and moody, his body precarious and threatening spill. The resemblance was shocking.

Ronan. I said it out loud for the first time in years, and it still had that feel to it, that moue of mouth halfway between pleasure and sorrow.

Ronan. Ronan McLeish. The chair righted itself as Dylan sounded the syllables, and his fingers tapped the keyboard. We waited for what might surface.

"He'll have changed," I said while I scanned the faces. "I would hardly know him." I had the presence of mind to keep my voice steady and my hands from clutching for my son.

I didn't think that Ronan could be netted on a social site — I had dabbled a few times, once after a bottle of wine, once after a truly awful blind date — and he was not to be found in any of the usual places. Dylan saw his name in a tourist directory instead, listed under chartered boat services and promising close encounters with seals.

"Seals?" smirked Dylan. "Freakin' hell, Mom. Is he some kind of hippie?" But I saw how his eyes had pulled to the name, and desperation made me devious.

"We could visit," I said. "We could do the big European trip together, check him out on the way. Hey, maybe he's got another family now, maybe you've got a Scottish stepbrother or two. Wouldn't that be random, Dilly?"

Dylan flinched, and I bought just the one ticket. I left Dylan with my mom and told her I was going to an international conference in Glasgow. My son stared at me; he'd never heard me dissemble before. At least not to another adult.

Ronan. There's a slow syncopation when I say it under my breath, like the slap of the sea against dock. The last of the sunlight catches the spume as the ferryman ties on. He shoves his hands into his pockets, then coughs and spits. I see that he's done with me. I grab my suitcase and pull it behind me, *badunk badunk* down the gangplank, conscious of his gaze. He's got the engine started before I reach the sand.

The lady at the bed and breakfast folds her arms over her cardigan when I ask for the seals.

"Ronan," she says, "It's him you're wanting. You'll need to be sharp tomorrow morning. Ronan runs smartly no matter if the tourists come. The seals are his, you know? A right blether he has with them, but he's always back for the first round at the Blue Man. And still there for last bell, if you know what I mean. You cannot have come for the seals, surely?

Have you relations on the island?" Her arms unfold and her cardigan droops open. I stay quiet. She sighs. "Aye well. Ronan tells a fine story. When he's in the mood."

She presses a leaflet into my hands the next morning. It's written in some ornate old script, pure theme pub kitsch, and probably what the tourists expect. The name of the boat knots with his own.

I find the *Selkie Maid*, but there's no sign of Ronan. A seagull steps along the dock, with one bright yellow eye turned in my direction. I settle myself on a bollard. My hands are clammy despite the morning sun.

He must have changed. But I can't picture how. I have him in mind as he was, and I've held him like that for years. I doubt he did the same for me. He would hardly know me now.

Dylan laughs at the photos of me from school. Morbid Michelle with hair jet-black and crimped, eyes soot-ringed and sullen. I wasn't one of the cheerleaders, with their teased highlights and lip gloss smiles. *Call me Shell*, I told them then, imagining something razor-edged against the skin.

"Shell," said Ronan, when he knew me better, "a delicate thing. Pale pink and sounding of the sea. You'll keep your pearl well hidden, won't you?"

It sounded better in his accent. No one talked like him, no one understood the power of delivery, of the soft lilt and dark-eyed glance.

He'd arrived in the last year of secondary school, in the middle of winter while the sea storms rattled the glass and tore needles off the firs, and he was always cold. He stood alone in the smoke pit and went through cigarette after cigarette, pale-faced and shivering in his ridiculous yellow coat. We knew he was from Scotland, a country that seemed lacking in both edge and pleasure, and faintly associated with the hard toffee and tartan-packaged shortbread our grannies sent at Christmas. We knew he was from some fluidly named island in that country, which we made him pronounce again and again, along with the words *murder* and *water* and *home*. The girls giggled and watched, waiting to see if he was cool.

He was not. He was thin and dark and prickly intense, a restless boy who rocked back in his chair and stared at nothing. Sometimes the wind would come in from the coast, bringing with it a hint of salt, and Ronan would tilt his head as if listening for something. His chair would scrape back and empty then, and we'd run to the window overlooking the playing field. There he'd be, wheeling and turning with his fingers spread to the wind, his coat pooled bright where he'd dropped it.

The jeers started soon after and Ronan smiled. He told the football captain that his neck was thicker than a bullock's and he called the pretty girls a bourach of snotty mingers. The hockey players swung at his long hair and pallor and threatened to kick his foreign arse all the way back to fairy land. Ronan shrugged off the blood and slipped away to his auntie's house. She was the town librarian, a spinster who sang in the church choir and wore odd tweed skirts. We mimicked her clasped hands and rolling r's, and she was another strike against him.

"It was a terrible shock, him turning up on my doorstep," she whispered to my mom. "But there was nothing for it. The mother ran off and he's just lost his da, and he has no other kin willing to claim him."

Of course I needed to know him. I loved his voice and his history and the way his wrist bones jutted when he reached.

The seagull plonks his yellow feet on the wooden slats of the dock. I watch the waves slap against the moorings and wish for a cigarette, even though it's been years since I quit. There's a hitch as someone steps down the gangplank, and the seagull flaps its wings and screeches, its red mouth gaping.

I turn, my breath suspended.

He's filled out and coarsened. He looks salted, years older than he should be, and his eyes are hooded with flesh. The turn of his mouth remains the same. He could be a mythic warrior or sea-weathered drunk; he could be any of the men I've seen in this place. I can see nothing of Dylan in him.

"I'm here for the seals," I say, and the seagull screeches again.

He looks me over like he's dragging something from memory and I tense, waiting for my name to surface.

"You'll take a small," he says, and throws me a lifejacket.

He steps onto the boat without a backward glance and busies himself with the engine. I clamber on after him, wondering how many customers he gets and whether they consider his terseness part of the local character. We set out and I lean into the wind, remembering Dylan when he was young and we travelled to the island, how he'd poke his face through the ferry railing to catch the spray and lick the salt from his lips after. How he would not come easily from the waves, and would slip shrieking from my grasp until I wound him in a beach towel with a promise of fish and chips from the fry shack.

"How was the trip?" Ronan calls to me over the noise of the motor. "Was it rough coming in?"

"A bit," I say. "Such a long drive to get here, nothing but sheep and potholes, and I'm in this little rental car, which the ferryman tells me I can't take on board. So I leave it parked and the crossing is so choppy that I — "

Ronan grunts. "It keeps the world away."

He cuts the engine when we come to a little cove and the boat rocks gently back and forth in the current. I peer into the water and Ronan leans back against the railings. We wait.

The water rolls green and opaque and I wish for something to throw into it. Dylan once made a boat from his fish and chips carton and floated it on the waves, and watched for it long after it bobbed into oblivion. *Not gone*, he insisted, *not gone just because you can't see it. Not gone, because everything comes back on the tide.*

Ronan is rubbing his thumbs against his fingers, as if he's needing a cigarette, or a drink.

"We tell a story here," he says. "There's a dark-eyed boy, a son of the village. He has a mother and a father, like any boy should, but this boy is different. This one's a listener. The storms call him to sea one night and he's lost. The villagers go looking, but there's nothing to find but a pile of clothes on the sand. Years pass. The boy is forgotten. One day a man washes ashore. Not a stitch on him. Flapping about like a seal pup, and barking, like this."

I laugh at the noises Ronan makes. But his eyes are on me now and my throat's closing.

"Ah Christ," he says and turns away. Thumb over finger, again and again.

"What then?" I ask to keep him talking. "What happened to the boy? When he was a man, I mean."

Ronan looks at me. I see that the skin around his eyes has softened and pouched, and his cheeks are traced with a delicate broken red.

"He goes back to the sea," he says. "They always do."

He turns his back on me and for a while there's nothing but the susurration of waves breaking on rock. I swallow, and think of the dark-eyed boy tilting his head towards sea. Ronan doesn't tell it like he used to but I remember the tale, and how his hands slid over my skin as he spoke. How his words could soothe.

Will I tell you about the selkie? Gentle things. They sing the sailors from the storm, you know? Out there, calling. My dad says there's this stretch of silver sand, that's where they slip off their skins to dance. Between sea and shore, and belonging truly to neither.

Underneath the birches and behind the bleachers, his hands would tug at my clothes and I would panic, unnerved by the open lacework of branches.

But if you find a sealskin cloak draped over rock? Ah. Then they're yours.

A button loosened or a t-shirt pushed up and my breath, hitched in.

Hide that skin and they'll stay. But always looking out to sea, you know? Yours for a time, but the sea will call them back. My dad says.

But I always stopped his hands. Not here, not now, I said. Not where everyone can see.

"Look!"

My belly rises as the waves rock the boat.

"Look," shouts Ronan again, his voice higher and younger. I follow his pointing finger to the sleeked heads: three, then four and more breaking the surface, gathering and nudging like children for a story. Ronan smiles and murmurs something in another language. He pushes a cooler box towards us and pries it open. The silvery scales flash and I remember the sunlight dappling through new leaves, and him haloed with it while he pulled me onto the damp grass. He grabs a fish and his hands on that slippery flesh are disconcerting, too intimate. I look away, busying myself with my phone.

Ronan throws the fish to the seals while I aim the phone at the dark velvet eyes and baby faces, wanting something to take back to Dylan. Ronan ignores me; he's speaking to his seals now in that throaty murmur, coaxing the smaller ones forward. He gestures towards the fish and I take one in my hands. It's sinuous under my touch and I let it slide into the water.

My graduation dress was made of deep blue satin that slipped over my legs as I walked. I sashayed up and down the hall and my mother sighed at its long trailing skirt, its mournful hue. I didn't care; I was a gothic mermaid.

I sat tangled in its folds as the music pulsed. The others danced while Ronan and I passed a mickey of vodka under the crepe-covered table, my hand touching his then brushing his thigh as the alcohol kicked in. Ronan grew moody and pushed back his chair. I followed him outside, past the bleachers and through the birches, to where the leaves grew lush. My dress floated above my hips like waves and I didn't care, I let him crash against me while the stars spun in a queasy spiral. He sunk his face in my hair after and cried. From love, I thought then.

Ronan smacks the cooler lid shut. "Cheer'ee," he says to the bobbing heads.

The seals turn and roll towards shore and the water ripples behind them.

"Cheer'ee ma ha." He raises his hand briefly, then clumps towards the cabin. I look for the place where the seals have been, but the surface has calmed to glass. There's no sign of them.

Ronan left before the leaves fell from our hiding place. The salt wind came in from the east and my belly swelled and pulled towards it. My parents went to talk to his auntie. She clasped her hands and said she would do anything she could, but Ronan? What could she do about him? He was never really hers, no matter the blood.

She sends a card for Dylan's birthday every year. It contains a handwritten wish and a crisp twenty dollar bill.

The cabin door slams and Ronan comes to lean over the railing, close enough for me to catch the sharpness of alcohol on him. I'm aware of him watching me. My breath stops, my lips lock tight on the question.

"Cheer'ee ma ha, my arse," he murmurs, "Look at you. Not understanding a bloody thing I say, and happier for it." His eyes darken. "Do you know that, Shell?"

I flush, and his eyes glint before he looks to the sea. The wind's coming up. He spreads his fingers to catch it and I see something of the boy in him then.

"Will I tell you something true?" he says. "Will I tell you about my father?"

He's speaking in his old voice now, the words lilting and rolling in the old rhythm.

Something breaks and splashes behind us, and Ronan glances at the rocks before

The sea breaks against the boat, whisper soft, and he lowers his voice. My skin.

"My father wore a bright yellow oilskin. Easy to see, even in the dark."

There's only the shushing of sea and my breath, hitched in.

They said my father had been clumsy with drink and lost his footing. That my father was gone for good."

And then Ronan turns to look at me. Just like he always did, when he knew I was hooked, when he knew I would follow him.

"He's out there. I like to think that, you know? Safe with the selkie." His hand swipes at his eyes and he laughs, short and sharp.

There's time then, while the mist comes in and the sea swells and slides, and Ronan lights a cigarette. I slow my breath and he turns away to exhale, his hands resting loosely on the railing. The saltwater has brined them; they could be scaled.

I tell him what I've come to say.

The mist has fallen by the time we reach dock. A seagull calls out, its voice muted and flat, and I see it sitting on a bollard with one leg tucked into its feathers. "My son," Ronan asks, "what's his name?"

Dylan. He turns it over in his mouth.

"He'd see you," I say. "If you wanted."

"Maybe," he says, "maybe." His hands shake as they light another cigarette. "Ah, I don't know. Maybe not. Maybe you should tell Dylan I'm lost." He exhales and his gaze floats over me to the village, to the pub with its garish blue sign. It's late afternoon and he has somewhere to be.

He leaves me standing on the dock. "Tell him I'll think of him," he calls, "when I'm out there. Tell him that."

I will. I'll tell Dylan how the seals look like lost children and how his father can murmur, how the mist comes between that place and ours. I'll tell him how a selkie slipped from its skin will never hold to land, for all the pretty words.

My dark-eyed son will shrug and go back to his computer, to the photos I've sent him.

I'll see how he stares at the sleek heads and velvet eyes, how he rubs at his skin like it itches.

How his head tilts like he's listening for something.

MEAT

"IS HE SLEEPING?"

My brother's pudgy hand stroked the long flank from haunch to shoulder, patted the head as you would a dog. There was a line of crusted blood along the mouth and a dark red cavity where the innards should be.

"He's dead, you retard," I said.

Alan's baby mouth trembled and Dad shot me a look. His arm went around my shoulder and I felt its weight.

"Give thanks," he said. "He died so we can eat."

The deer hung in the barn for a week. I took Alan into the dusty dark to look at the body strung up by the antlers, at the ribcage split open. There was a small hole just under the jaw and the fur had gone black around it. It looked like the stubbed out end of a cigarette.

"That's where the bullet went in," I said. "Bet you won't touch it."

Alan kneeled, and poked at the little drops of blood spattered on the cement floor.

I stuck my little finger into the hole, to prove that I could. Scabby, hard, like picking your nose after a bad bleed. Alan wasn't looking; the ants had found the scatter of blood and were doing a frenzied dance, and he'd settled back on his haunches to watch. I circled the hanging body with my feet Indian soft. My hands cupped a rifle, my eye squinted through the scope and it was real, so real I could feel the buttplate denting my shoulder and my finger tensing on the trigger, so real I could see the five-point buck in the underbrush, all cagey smart. Step, step, and the buck lifted its head, ready to bolt. My finger pulled. Pow. Dead eye and better than Dad.

Alan stood up. "I won't eat him," he said.

And he didn't. Mom made him macaroni and cheese while we crammed venison burgers into our mouths, and Dad laughed at the smear of ketchup on my chin and gave me a swallow of beer straight from the bottle.

The deer fed us through winter. The brown paper parcels thawed on a plate next to the sink and left puddles of watery blood. The black-marked labels were spare as bone. RIB, SHOULDER, HAUNCH. A leathery raw smell filled the house when the meat cooked and Dad told us to breathe deep, for this was an honest stink. You knew what you were eating with deer. You knew it had lived. Alan would gag and refuse, and Dad would insist he join hands and pray anyway.

For meat. That we should eat when others have none.

I got my first real rifle the summer I turned thirteen: a pump action Winchester like Dad and his dad before him. The forestock made a satisfying click when I slid it back. I looked through the crosshairs and aimed the empty gun at the fencepost and the cows and my brother. Dad said I was old enough to learn gunmanship and took me to the shooting range.

My first lesson was a watermelon.

"Draw a face on it," said Dad. "Make it look like your brother." He handed me the Jiffy marker he used when he butchered.

I squinted up my eyes against the sun and drew long lashes and a lolling tongue, because my brother collected butterflies and studied the stars and he was a total pansy-ass retard.

Dad propped the watermelon on the target bench while I loaded the rifle. I knew to wait until he was clear, I knew to line up through the notch and down slightly because I clustered high on a target. The heat left wavering lines around the bench and my hands sweated on the gunmetal. A fly buzzed around my ear.

A crack and echo. The target bench stood empty.

We retrieved half of the watermelon from the weeds. It smiled up at me, a pulp of red flesh where the eyes should be and the drawn-on tongue jagged and torn. The other half was spattered against the tree trunks. The flies were already clustering. I swallowed down the thing closing my throat.

"Never aim at another person. You got that?" said Dad. He unloaded my gun and pocketed the cartridges.

We stopped for ice-cream on the way back. Tiger stripe for Dad and strawberry swirl for me, and Mr Cooper behind the counter asked how's the hunting and did we bag anything and did we need more ammo?

"Not today," Dad said. "We got ice-cream today and that's enough."

❦

Dad took me hunting every October, when the bush had gone quiet and gold and the crunch of twigs underfoot sounded like dry shot. We'd light a fire when the sun sunk low. The water would boil in the old army pot and I'd bitch and moan; whole day gone and nothing killed, nothing. Dad would tell me to wait. That I'd get a deer next time because God knew I wasn't ready now.

When I was fifteen I shot a doe. Clean, right above the eye. She dropped like a dream.

And I was too puffed up to speak when we stopped for ice-cream, and Mr Cooper saw the body strung to the rack and popped a beer, and Dad passed the bottle to me.

Alan came running when we pulled into the driveway. Hale-Bopp, he was saying, it was all over the news and you could see it without a telescope and Mom said it was okay but ask Dad. So could he? Could he stay up late and watch for it, with church tomorrow and all?

"We'll stay up," said Dad. "No greater church than nature."

Dad came to my room later with a flashlight and blanket. I sat up and squinted at him.

"You're doing this for a stupid comet?"

"Not just any stupid comet. Hale-Bopp."

"Hale whatever," I said. "I got a deer today, you remember that? A deer's real, it's something you can eat, and you're letting Alan freak out about a comet?"

"You're both my sons," said Dad.

But I knew. I knew I was the one he took hunting.

Meat

I failed at school and I was too slow for fast food, and I hated the boredom of working at the mill. But I excelled at basic training. My uniform collar was straight, I marched in time and I could run an eight minute mile in full gear. They didn't make me do a hundred push-ups like they did in the movies, but I could, and my gun was well-oiled and by my side at all times.

They let us go home for Thanksgiving before we shipped out to Kandahar.

I sat at the table in my uniform. It wasn't strictly necessary; Mom had left my bedroom untouched and the closet was still hung with my old clothes. But I liked what the uniform said about me, that I'd been tested and approved and was now part of something bigger than this family. That I was out in the world doing something important. Alan sat across from me with his nut roast. He was in the last year of his teaching degree and a total save-the-world retard.

"So," he said. "You all ready to fight the good fight?"

"Yes sir," I said. I spooned a hole into my mashed potatoes and waited for gravy.

"And the women and children?" he asked. "What about them?"

"We're there to protect them. We're there to bring them democracy."

"By carpet bombing them?"

The sergeant had told us that the civilians wouldn't get what we were doing.

Especially the educated ones. "It's about extremists. We're going to stop the extremists. You remember that thing called 9/11?"

"You think that was extremists?" he said. "You think the government didn't know?"

And I could have leaned over the table and pinned him face down in his whole-grains, mussed up that gelled hair, knocked some sense into his stupid head. Christ knows I could have but didn't because Mom said "Stop it boys, not at dinner," and Dad took my hand. My brother's wrists were skinny as a girl's anyway.

I closed my eyes while Dad asked for God's grace in this, and in everything we should do away from His light, in the countries of the oppressed and the starving and the violent, in the countries where brother fought brother.

I managed to get home in time to change into my civilian clothes the next Thanksgiving. The feel of soft cotton against my ribcage unnerved me, and the way the house smelled like laundry detergent made my chest tighten. The pattern of the kitchen wallpaper, the same sunny swirls I'd traced my finger around when I was a kid, seemed to jump at me when I turned my back. I knew I was eating too fast so I cut channels between my turkey and carrots and stuffing. It looked more like a canteen tray that way.

"Total battle zone," Alan was saying. He'd begun his first job at an inner-city school.

"There's a metal detector at the front door so the kids can't bring in knives."

I nodded. Yeah, I knew about that, about the kids. There was that one came into our camp, a skinny teenager with big dark eyes and reaching hands, saying Please please so that I can eat and Private Johnson tossed him a package of saltines and the boy just stood there looking at us. Then the sergeant shot him in the head and Private Johnson puked and we found the homemade explosives wired to the boy's skinny chest before we shovelled the sand over him.

"You okay, son?" said Dad.

I stopped swirling my food and remembered to bring the fork to my mouth. The taste was good; it was far away from the flies and the canvas and the sand that got everywhere, and it was nothing like the long spells we spent playing Call of Duty and drinking lukewarm Coke before the crack of a rifle snapped us to order.

"I'm good," I said. "Thankful." For this, for meat so that we might eat.

℧

Alan wrote me letters when I was in the desert. He wrote about the thirteen-year-olds who stole food for their families, and how the eyes of the tough girls glistened at the death of Juliet, and how they all thought Holden Caulfield was a pussy bitch retard. He wrote about the kids finding a fledgling crow and how they fed it scraps from the school canteen and called it Tupac.

And I thought of writing back. I thought about telling him about the boy and the saltines and how the sunset in the desert was as red as blood and bigger than any of us, and maybe there was something in that but I couldn't get what. I thought of writing but I never did.

Nothing looked right the next Thanksgiving. The swirls on the wallpaper bored into my eyes, and the edges of people's faces blurred when I turned my head too fast. I concentrated on the meat on my plate, on sawing it into smaller and smaller pieces.

The doctor said it was normal. Detachment after an incident, the numbness after deactivation. She said I should keep busy and focus on finding a job. The sergeant said that I shouldn't think about it; war was a different country and shit happened and nobody back home was going to understand that. Christ, he would've done the same if it was him that had been fired on, wouldn't have stopped to think about it, either. And take the pills. The pills were going to help in the days to come.

I said no to the turkey and yes to the stuffing because it tasted more green than rusty like blood, and Alan's girlfriend smiled at me. She was too skinny, with glasses and straight brown hair, but pretty when she smiled.

And Alan was talking, something about thirty faces filled with hatred because he was The Man coming in telling them how to live, the ones at the back saying go home bitch with their t-shirts raised to show metal, and he wanted to, he wanted to just pack up and leave because didn't know what he was doing there anyway. Yeah, he should just let them be, with their illiteracy and bad attitudes and homemade blades, and if they wanted to call that freedom so be it.

So Dad said the world has always been troubled and love will persevere, and Mom whispered amen and passed the gravy. And Alan knocked over his beer and the bottle hit his knife with a crack and my trigger finger pulled air.

The sergeant said it could have been anything, that crack and rattle, it could have been a Kalashnikov and it sounded just like it, and he would have done the same. That war was all about things lining up and no time to think, because thinking gets you killed damn quick. So the things that lined up that day — the sheet metal dumped by the building crew, the goats clambering over it — were nothing but they could have been something and what was a damn goat herd doing in the middle of a risk zone anyway? Still, it was some piece of shit. About the girl.

The beer puddled and dripped. Alan's girlfriend wiped away the stain.

"It's okay," she said, "it'll wash away. Don't cry."

❦

I got my old job back at the mill. I edged and trimmed the boards into lengths, and I kept my earmuffs tilted so the noise of the saws could scream through my head and cut out everything else. I ate my sandwiches by the river when the weather was good. My ears hummed and I thought of nothing, and I guess I was okay.

Alan didn't write as much. I got a few emails saying how the gangs had come in and how their tags got spray-painted on the canteen walls by kids with stolen guns. How he'd been asked to speak at two funerals and the teachers were walking the corridors in pairs, how they talked in the staffroom of Rugers or Glocks and which was best to carry, and how he wanted neither. I sat by the river and looked at his words on my phone, and sometimes I said them out loud because I liked the way they sounded.

The foreman motioned me over one Monday morning. I saw the look on his face and thought of the girl with the goats, I thought that he'd found out somehow and he figured my hands were too dirty for all that pale wood. But then he dropped his eyes and told me to go home, that my family would need me at a time like this.

Mom was in bed, sleeping off whatever the doctors had given her. Dad sat at the kitchen table, his hands folded together but his mouth silent. He nodded when I said I would go, that I should be the one who sees to Alan. I took my garment bag from the closet and unzipped it and put on my uniform.

The bus had a miniature TV screen mounted from the ceiling. The news came on and someone stood in front of a school, mouthing words. The camera swerved, slid over the parking lot and stopped on a car door hung open, its window glass shattered. No sound, but the words looped and spooled across the bottom of the screen. *Caught in the crossfire one police officer and three civilians.* A few armed guards, a crying woman with the tagline calling her a colleague, then a march of banners and placards from some other day, a sunnier place. *Blood on your hands, stop the NRA.*

And I closed my eyes because I couldn't see what any of this had to do with Alan.

The coroner nodded when he saw my uniform. He asked where I'd served and was it Helmand province because he'd heard it was bad over there, and was it okay if he shook my hand? If he told me that I was a real hero for protecting our freedom? He left me alone when I stayed silent.

My brother looked like he was sleeping, except for the sheet folded over the top of his head. I thought of the girl with the goats and the boy with the explosives and how we hadn't thought to do that, to cover what was gone, and the noise of the sawmill began in my head and stayed there when I signed the forms, when I took his wallet and his phone home in a plastic bag, when I told Dad it was done.

℮

Alan's girlfriend phoned a few times after the funeral. I nodded a lot while I pressed a cold beer to my forehead, and she couldn't hear what I was thinking so she stopped calling. Life went back to something. Not normal, but something.

℮

I still work at the mill. I eat my dinner at home so Dad can get Mom out of bed and Mom can pretend that the microwave meatloaf took all day to make. Dad still says grace and Mom still echoes him but sometimes he forgets a word while Mom smiles at her plate, and I'm no help because I got this hum in my head all the time now. I can't eat the meat anyway; the salty blood taste makes me gag. I know Dad thinks it has something to do with Alan. It doesn't.

If we have enough light left after dinner, we take the guns out. We don't hunt. We set up beer cans, or old apples and potatoes; whatever we got goes on the bench and we shoot it down. There's a comfort in the load and reload, the recoil, in the dry click of an empty chamber.

We don't go for ice-cream. Mr Cooper's been dead over a year now and the store sells frozen yogurt and eco-friendly cleaning products.

We lean against the fence after. The dusk settles around us. Sometimes Dad puts his arm around my shoulder and sometimes he doesn't. There's a rightness to the silence, a kind of peace in nothing much to say.

CRYPTODOME

MY SISTER STARTED SMOKING AT the end of March. Openly smoking that is. She'd been charming cigarettes off the boys since she'd shrugged herself into her first bra. My mother and I would watch her from the kitchen window while we washed the dinner dishes. Louette would stand under the streetlight with her kitten heels spiking the snow and her thin leather jacket left undone. The smoke rolled off her and plumed up to the moon. Her hand rose lazily to her mouth and the red ember flashed there like a hazard light. Then her hand would drift down, the sparks scattering from its fingers. That hand would still be warm when I passed her the dish towel later, and I would see her footprints in the snow the next morning, melted there amongst the fallen ash and frozen hard by the night's cold.

"Look at her," my mother said, "strutting around like she knows what it's all about. Just like me at the same age, and would you look at how that turned out. Chrissakes, would you just *look at her.*"

And you did look at her. You stared openly in the street or the mall or the school cafeteria, for you could not take your eyes off Louette. She'd flow into a space with her hips roiling and eyes arching and dark hair glowing red where it caught the light. Her mouth would curl into a smile, and you'd feel the oxygen sucked out of your lungs. Breathless, restless, waiting for something to happen, you'd look at her. She'd stand in the centre of the room and let the air rearrange itself around her. Her voice, when it came, was deep and smoky and you'd swear you were hearing some profound secret, even if she'd only stopped to ask the time.

"Don't you start up like her," my mom said with her hands shoved deep in the scalding dish water, "You're supposed to be the smart one. You still going to do that volcano?"

I nodded. The science fair was in June and the top contestant would go to the provincial finals in the city. I'd planned to set up a colour wheel and talk about light spectrums; I'd already painted the discs and spun their patterns to white in front of Louette and her boyfriend. Then the little earthquakes rattled through Washington State, shaking up the Americans just over the border and tearing a crack in their prettiest mountain. The smoke spewed straight up in a delicate stream and my science teacher passed me a book on Pompeii.

He said there could be an eruption, a real catastrophic event right here in our lifetime.

"Topical, this volcano," he said, "A real topical topic, Marie." His eyes glinted green as he leaned towards me, and I caught the fresh smell of his aftershave. My face burned red. Mr. Robson liked to play with words like that, liked to tease the girls with his jokes. I practiced all my best one liners for him behind the locked bathroom door, mouthing them to the mirror while the water ran.

"Mr Robson's hot," said Louette, her eyes half-lidded and her hand twisting her hair, "Don't you think so, Marie? Much too old for you, though." She laughed and reached for her cigarettes.

Smoking wasn't the only thing Louette had started. My mother would tell us to go to bed at a decent hour, then kiss us on our foreheads and swat at our butts before leaving for her shift at the truck stop cafe. The door would slam behind her. I'd pack my homework away at ten and prop myself up on pillow to watch Louette press the glossy red to her lips and mist her hair with drugstore scent. Then I'd hear the front door open and shut before I drifted off to sleep. Once, sometime after midnight, I woke to Louette's muffled curses while a trail of stale smoke and tinny beer wafted through our bedroom. The white of her boyfriend's hockey jacket bobbed and glowed where it caught the light.

"What's it like?" I whispered while she undressed in the dark. The hockey jacket hit the floor with a thunk.

"Who knows?" she said with her smoky laugh, "He says we should wait until we're married. Which means we park by the lake and look at the water for a while. Then we do everything but and I tell him to stop when he wants more." She laughed again, but I could hear something red hot churning under her words.

Louette had been going out with Stan for two years. Stan played goalie for the Laketown Flames and the pucks slid off him like rain off a mountain side. He was serious about Louette and had given her a ring. It wasn't a diamond. Engaged to be engaged, Louette announced to everyone while drifting the cubic zirconia in front of their faces.

The diamond would come later she said, once Stan had graduated high school and was working full time in his dad's auto repair shop. Stan would look at Louette while she talked, his face craggy and solid, his big hand clamped to her shoulder.

Stan had helped me paint the colour discs for my science project, back when I was still doing light spectrums. Hockey season had ended and he had some free time. He'd sat with his knees wedged underneath the kitchen table and his elbows spread square, and apply delicate strokes of colour to cardboard. I could do three wheels to his one. He never tired of sticking the discs on the motorised nail and watching the colours spin to oblivion.

"Weird," he'd said, "how the parts are so clear one minute. Green, red, blue: right there in front of you. Then you turn it and everything gets mixed up into nothing. Pure white. Like a face full of ice after a totally gruesome body check." It had taken him a while to adjust when I'd changed my topic. "Volcanoes?" he'd asked, "That's like smoke and danger, total destruction. Yeah I guess I can see why you'd want that. But this colour wheel, now it's just a real amazing thing, isn't it?" I'd let him paint a few more discs before I brought out the plans for the volcano.

Once he'd gotten used to the idea, Stan was the ideal partner. He cut and attached chicken wire while I mixed paste and tore strips of newspaper. He shaped the cone of the volcano and built up the layers. He advised on structure and dry times. He stuck little trees from his train set at the base of the volcano and added a tin foil lake, then plonked a plastic deer on the hillside. "For drama," he said, "When that volcano blows, it's gonna take out some lives. Gonna do some serious carnage." Louette wound herself around him then and whispered in his ear. I knew she was asking him if they could drive out to the lake. She was in a good mood today, all bubble and froth after a week of sullen silence. Stan smiled at me and unstuck his knees from under the table. His Camaro started up in a series of shotgun blasts while I was left scraping cold paste from newspaper.

Winter turned to spring. The snowdrifts yellowed and softened and the first of the pussy willows burst into cloud. The sky rippled between clear blue and swollen gray, and meltwater trickled off the roof and froze into spikes on the colder nights. Louette stormed around with her face drawn tight and her fingers itching towards her pack of cigarettes. She went out in bare arms and stood under street light with her skin radiating heat.

I plucked up my nerve and asked Mr Robson for advice on my topical topic. He told me to keep a journal, to watch the news and read the papers. Mount St. Helens was making headlines. *March 27th . . . copied . . . There is a swarm of earthquakes, one of them registering five point one on the Richter scale and carving out a crater before bringing an avalanche. Then comes an ash column, sent seven thousand feet into the air and falling within a twelve mile radius. March 29th: a second crater appears. There is visible flame, and static electricity sends out lightning bolts two miles long. April 5th: there are at least five earthquakes a day and the governor declares a state of emergency.*

My mother returned early from her shift one night . . . her ulcer was acting up again . . . and caught Louette sneaking in through the back door. "Chrissakes, girl," she said with one hand on the kitchen counter and the other clutching her gut. "Why should he pay for milk when he can get the cow for free?"

Louette stared at her with her black eyes smoking and her cheeks flushed scarlet, but said nothing.

My mother filled a glass with water and dropped two tablets into it. They fizzed and frothed and we all watched. "You're on the narrow road to not much," she said as she shuffled to her bedroom. "Believe me girl, I know."

Louette mouthed the words at me, threw her hands in the air and wiggled her boobs and hips for emphasis.

It was hard to resist her when she was like this. I laughed and we shimmied around the kitchen, Louette sing-songing under her breath: the narrow road, the narrow road to not much.

But Louette was grounded for the entire month of April and I was made her guardian. She made a point of smoking inside and leaving her butts in the plant pots. Stan came over to apologise to my mother. He stood in the kitchen with his big hands hanging and his face wobbling, and waited until my mother told him to go away. Louette brought her biology text book home from school and sat cross-legged on her bed, drawing cycles and spirals on blank paper. Photosynthesis, she wrote, and made the dot on the letter i into smiling sun. I told her it looked dumb and she told me to mind my own business. She helped me paint my volcano, dipping a brush into red and dragging it down the side of the mountain. "You ever think about this place?" she said. "About where we live?"

"It's okay," I said, concentrating on gluing down the trees.

"We live in a goddamn trailer park," said Louette, "You and me? We're trailer trash.

We live in a shitty trailer park in the shittiest part of a shithole town. This is not okay."

The volcano sat between us, glistening with paint, and I could see how the newsprint had smudged gray underneath, how the entire structure looked shabby and cheap despite our work.

"I'm going to get out of here," said Louette softly. She pinched the paintbrush between her fingers and its end glowed ember red.

Louette helped me wrap the volcano in a black plastic garbage bag and carry it to school. We delivered it to the science room and Mr Robson stood up when we came in. "Louette," he said, "How's the dark cycle going?" Louette smiled as he lifted the bag off us, and his green gaze wavered from her eyes to her lips. I stood silent while they talked of biphosphate and glyceraldehyde and glucose, and who Louette liked to hang out with and what music she liked to listen to. I could feel the lip gloss I'd put on earlier sticking to my mouth like glue.

April 21st . . . I wrote in my journal that night . . . Mount St. Helens continues to cause concern. Scientists have noticed harmonic tremors on their instruments. They think the magma under the mountain is on the move.

Stan was finally allowed to visit. The Camaro pulled up with its engine blatting and my mother called down the hall. Louette sat perfectly still with her eyes gone dark. Stan's voice stammered at the door and Louette gave me a small tight smile before she grabbed her cigarettes and sauntered away. She didn't glance in the mirror before she went; her lips were left unglossed and her hair hung lifeless.

Stan seemed as rock solid as always on the surface, but I saw the changes. He sat at our kitchen table and tried to talk to me. I poured him a cola and waited. "Something's changed," he said, watching the bubbles fizz and rise, "Louette's all different." His face worked then, his mouth twisted and his forehead bulged and I was terrified he might burst into tears.

"It's just school," I said quickly with my mind casting around for details. "Final exams and all, you know? Especially biology. She can never remember the difference between light and dark reactions. Mr Robson is helping her."

Mr Robson was helping both of us. He handed me a tin of baking soda and a little glass flask of vinegar and told me to mix the two together. The foam frothed over test-tube edge and Louette laughed in throaty surprise. "An acid and base reaction," said Mr Robson, "Pure chemistry when those two meet, and the results are explosive." His green eyes glinted as they slid from me to Louette. I sat at the high laboratory table and experimented with proportions of bicarbonate and vinegar and red food colouring, recording my observations in my volcano journal. The mixture needed to erupt perfectly on the day of science fair; it would have to bubble up the test-tube hidden in the paper-mache dome and pour down the sides, suggesting fiery magma to my awestruck audience. I watched Mr Robson lean over Louette and guide her pencil around his drawing of the Kreb's cycle, and I remembered how he smelled up close, as fresh and mossy as the forest after rain. Louette turned towards him and her eyes widened a little, and I thought she'd probably just noticed the same thing.

April 30th. The United States Geological Survey reports that one side of the mountain is bulging. This is from the pressure of the magma building inside. 270 feet of rock shifted now, and more pushed out every day.

May came and Louette's detainment lifted. Stan showed up at the door with a big loose grin and his car keys jangling, telling us how pretty the lake looked with sun on it. Louette told him she was studying. I watched his face change shape, the muscles underneath his skin shifting and setting to stoic silence.

"Later, maybe?" she whispered, and his face softened.

I was woken again in the early hours by the bedroom door creaking open. It was too warm now for the hockey jacket, but Louette's skin glowed white where she'd bared it. She sat on the edge of her bed, just sat there silent and still, and I turned towards her. The usual smoky vapour drifted from her but something had changed; she smelled of some other thing both sweet and sharp. I thought of leaves unfurling and mossy rock and fallen rain, I sensed the colour green twisting through the dark and winding tight around my guts.

"Go back to sleep," Louette whispered, "You're dreaming this."

May 7th. The eruptions have started again. They are small. You can't see the magma boiling away underneath the solid rock. This is called a cryptodome. Crypto means hidden.

Mount St. Helens was in the news regularly now. It had become a familiar face, and it showed up in the comic strips smiling and blowing puffy clouds into blue sky. The tourists ate hot dogs and pointed their cameras at the ash plume, the cabin owners snuck into the danger zone and came out with porch chairs and bed frames piled into the backs of their pickup trucks. The geologists squinted at the cameras and spoke about the rate of intrusion and the resulting instability, and shrugged when the reporters asked when. The volcanologists threw their hands around and thrust jagged seismic graphs at the newspapers.

"Yeah it looks calm but what's happening underneath is the important thing. And, whoo boy, this could be *big*," said one. "The entire north face could slide, and if that happens we'll have a full scale catastrophe on our hands."

Louette seemed to sleepwalk through those days, slow and barely there, like some of her fire had gone out. She mumbled and drifted around the place, half dressed and half awake and always with a cigarette dangling. It often smouldered forgotten but she seemed to need the weight of it there in her hand. Night would come and something would spark in her eyes, and I got used to the empty bed on her side of the room.

Stan dropped by on the Friday before it happened. I was home alone. Louette had cornered me in the school corridor and said she would be late, that she wanted to finish off something at school.

"Where is she?" Stan asked. He stood in the kitchen doorway with his arms hanging empty and his chest caving inwards, but his face looked swollen, ready to burst. I could feel that awful tightness on my own face when I answered.

"With Mr Robson," I said, as if it were nothing. I heard the Camaro spin away, throwing gravel like a fistful of rage, and I had to sit down for the shaking in my knees.

Saturday was quiet. Mount St. Helens had ceased all visible activity and the news was filled with Cuban refugees and race riots and the number 1 hit single by a sharp-cheeked blonde, who looked a lot like Louette without the darkness. In the calm, the tourists had gone home and the cabin owners were officially allowed to collect their belongings. Louette drifted through the rooms, picking up things and putting them down again.

"Stan?" she said when I asked, "No. I saw the Camaro in the student lot, but I never saw Stan. I should call him, I guess." She looked at the phone and picked up her cigarettes instead.

Sunday May 18th was Mother's Day. Louette and I were up early; I'd volunteered at the Strawberry Brunch held in the school cafeteria every year, and Louette had decided to come along. Our mother slipped in at seven just as she always did after a night shift, and told us she'd see us there after a few hours of sleep.

By twenty minutes past eight, I was setting places on the pink-clothed cafeteria tables and Louette was slicing strawberries into a bowl. Mr Robson was supervising the kids and staff that year. He hummed as he propped test-tubes of coloured water and carnations at each table, and neither he nor Louette looked at one another. The students bustled back and forth with trays of cold cuts and baking powder biscuits, Louette licked her fingers and the kitchen staff gossiped while they worked.

At eight thirty there was a displacement of air. Nothing more than that, no explosion or sonic boom or blast of smoke, just a sudden quiet that made me set down my stack of plates and look up.

Stan stood in the cafeteria doorway with a shotgun hanging from his hands. His eyes bulged and glared in his swollen face, like they were about to pop from some force within, and he was panting. The silence echoed through the room, bouncing off the twelve-grader clutching her throat to the hockey captain in mid-cower to the kitchen worker staring over her pot of steaming water. Louette held out her hands and they were stained red from the strawberries, but Stan was not looking at her. He raised the gun.

Mr Robson stared back. He was holding a test tube and I saw how the carnations trembled in their crimson water. I saw how the colour had seeped into their delicate folds, tracing the red there like veins, and I swallowed hard.

"It was nothing," he said, "Nothing. It meant nothing to me."

Several things happened all at once then. Stan moved faster than I would have ever thought possible, breaking from doorway and towards Mr Robson with steps like stumbling boulders, the shotgun wedged to his shoulder. *No no no* said someone and *please* said another and there was the gurgling cough of the hockey captain retching. The kitchen worker dropped her pot of hot water and it splashed and steamed and Mr Robson cried out. Stan moved fast but

Louette moved faster, lifting the bowl of strawberries high and throwing it full force into Stan's face.

Eight thirty two. I remember how my eyes spun from bleeding carnations to blank dinner plates to the ticking clock face, instinctively thinking to record the time. I watched the second hand tremble and freeze and take an eon to click forward.

Stan wheeled back and smacked against the wall, sliding down it almost gracefully. The bowl bounced beside him and the mashed berries and red juice dripped from his cheek, spreading across cafeteria floor. His face crumpled and collapsed and he began to weep. The shotgun hung balanced across his skewed knees for a moment before it clattered to the tiles. Someone moaned, then there was absolute silence.

Louette stood facing Stan with her hair come undone and her sweater pulled off one shoulder. We looked at her, we stared until her image wavered and blurred and burnt itself into our eyes. Louette stood still while the air around her roiled and sparked, and we could not take our eyes off her.

"The ring," someone whispered, "She's not wearing his ring."

My eyes slid from Louette's bare finger to the glint of gold lying next to strawberrystained knife, and my hand went out before I could stop it, cupped around the ring and held it inside my fist. The ring, his ring; the whisper went around the room like a wave and I knew I'd kept something safe.

"Pathetic," said Louette then. I saw how her eyes swerved to Mr Robson and stayed there, I saw how Mr Robson looked away. Louette laughed, short and sharp and caustic as ground glass. She turned on her heel and walked out.

I found her outside dragging deep on a cigarette.

"I should quit this shit," she said, "I don't even like the taste."

We missed the eruption of St. Helen's that day. At eight thirty two a.m., a five point one earthquake sheared off the side of the mountain and sent it hurtling down river valley at one hundred and fifty five miles per hour. The resulting landslide displaced the contents of an entire lake, splashing its water six hundred feet up and hillside and toppling the surrounding forest. The magma boiling inside the cryptodome for so long found itself exposed to the air, and it reacted instantly, exploding massive amounts of rock debris, volcanic gas, ash and pumice. The landslide was quick, but the magma was quicker; it overtook the slide at speeds of six hundred and eighty miles per hour, breaking the sound barrier. It vapourised everything in an eight mile radius and its superheated clouds blasted the foliage off trees many miles beyond that. Fifty seven people were killed, most of them asphyxiated. Some were burnt. Some were buried.

We missed the eruption, but they had started showing the footage on the television by the time we got home from the police station. The smoke billowed a dirty gray and I handed Louette her ring. Her fist closed around it but she did not put it back onto her finger. We watched the ash spew and Louette let me hold her hand. It was small and cold in mine.

The eruption sent an ash column twelve miles up and the air currents swirled it down again, covering thousands of miles in a caustic blanket and blacking out the noonday sun. The mudslides grated across bridges and the acid rain burnt the evergreen paint off the Washington state road signs. The ash flew across the border and we watched our clear blue sky darken by degrees. There was a fine grey dust covering the tops of the cars by the next morning. No one went to school, even though it was a Monday.

The police let Stan go after a few days of questioning. His father paid the fines and the police handed him back his gun. Stan was expelled from school and forbidden from graduating that year. None of us saw him for weeks and the rumours swirled and spread, dirtying the mouth with their taste. Some of that gossip grazed Louette, but she brushed it off like she didn't care.

My volcano journal lay unopened and I stopped going to science class. A garbage bag showed up on our doorstep the week before the science fair, with a note attached. I took the paper-mache volcano out of the black plastic, and threw the note away with the bag.

I was not surprised to see the science fair hall steaming with homemade volcanoes, all in various states of frothy eruption. The room filled with the bitter stench of vinegar while the kid with the colour wheel spun his plates to white. The judge pinned a blue ribbon to his stall and I was not surprised by this either.

The ash fell down and got swept up, and eventually dispersed to farther places. It was decided that Louette carried no blame for what happened; a relationship outgrown, an engagement ring handed back and a young man left broken-hearted. It was only natural, for Louette was beautiful. And working surprisingly hard at her studies these days. Hadn't she been getting extra help with her biology before the volcano blew? Louette walked the corridors with her hips roiling and her head held high, and the younger girls began showing up to school with dishevelled hair and their sweaters hanging off their shoulders. Louette brushed that off too and circled job vacancies at the back of the city newspapers.

Mount St. Helens erupted a few more times throughout the summer and fall, and the ash circled the globe, turning up as far away as Helsinki. We all got used to the taste of it at the back of our throats. It snowed black that winter and Stan drove to the lake with his father's shotgun lying on the passenger seat of his Camaro. Mr. Robson spoke on behalf of the school at the funeral. He didn't mention the volcano; he talked about flowers in the field instead. I saw the crimson veins of carnations, the blood-red water, and had to choke back the bile. Louette called to say she'd seen the snow on the news and was it really as black as that? She was working as a medical receptionist in a wealthier part of Vancouver by then, and dating a doctor.

Mount St. Helens settled, the lilies pushed through the ash piles and the sparrows perched on fledgling saplings. The years passed and I went away to university, while my sister grew tired of dating and married a cardiologist. He made her quit smoking when she turned forty. Now I work in seismic research and plot data on tidy graphs, and when I emerge blinking from the departmental basement, I have the sense of keeping something safe.

Mount St. Helens still vents steam and ash once in a while, and Louette phones me every time. "Turn on the TV," she'll say, "you don't want to miss it."

I can hear the restlessness in her voice, that sense of breathy excitement that still draws people to her. I know how her hands will hum with heat while her fingers flutter and tap, searching for a long ago cigarette to light and suck to a red hot ember. My sister talks of her pretty children while I tell her about my research and we never say how, on a certain kind of spring morning, we wake with the taste of ash in our mouths.

PURPLE MARTIN

YEAH, I KNOW. I KNOW I'm not supposed to drive cuz I'm thirteen and three years away from being legit, I know it goddamn well. But some things go beyond legit. Some things just gotta be done and to hell with how it's supposed to be.

So this is how I come to roll the old Chevy out of the barn after Mom and Dad leave to make the hospital arrangements. This is why I stand with the keys in my hand, looking at the sunlight glinting off the chrome. It's August, and the swallows are going hellbent for leather, turning and flashing above my head. If I had my BB gun I'd knock them right out of the sky. It's August, and my eyes burn and my armpits smell as sharp as a roadkill skunk.

We're supposed to be barefoot and skinny-dipping in the lake, but we're not. Not this year.

I slide in behind the Chevy's wheel. Yeah, I'm not supposed to drive but I know how, I been practising with Dad since I was ten. The engine grinds when I crank her up and I don't think she's gonna catch but then she does, and I sit for a while with my hands sweating on the wheel. When I turn off the ignition, the silence hangs hot and heavy. I go and get Marty.

He's awake. Mom's left the curtain open a little, and the sun comes in on a lightsaber beam over the Star Wars action figures lined up on the windowsill, the ones I gave Marty but he hardly plays with anymore. It's August, and he's still under a double layer of blankets. His room stinks of stale wool and something worse.

He's got his head turned to one side and his eyes half-closed in that way he has now, but his gaze swivels when I grab his foot through the covers and give it a good shake.

"Sheeit, Marty," I say, "glorious goddamn day and you snoozing it away. Sheeit."

And Marty smiles, cuz he likes it when I swear like one of the hay crew on a smoke break, when I draw the word out between my teeth and roll it around my mouth, like we got all the time in the world.

He's six, same as I was when he was born. Six, and summer should be all blue sky and long day and no goddamn idea of anything else.

"Hey Marty," I say, "you wanna go to the lake?"

He watches me like he's trying to see if I'm jerking him around but then he nods. I help him to the toilet, telling him to do a pee before we go and he tries but not much comes out. I dig out his sneakers from last summer and they still fit. I try not to think about that while I tie the laces for him cuz he's never learned how. Forever tripping over his trailing feet and falling on his baby soft ass and, yeah, me laughing cuz it was funny the retarded look he got the second before his face crumpled.

"Ooh," I'd say, flapping my hands like a spastic, "Marty's a *special boy.*"

But now he can hardly walk so I piggyback him down the stairs and out the door, and prop him up in the passenger seat of the Chevy. I'm not totally shit-for-brains; I bring his hat and a blanket no matter the heat, and I click his seatbelt closed and yank it twice just to make sure.

Marty watches me with his eyes squinted up against the sun. He's breathing hard through his mouth, whistling a little bit. His breath stinks. His gums bleed and he won't let Mom brush his teeth anymore, not even with a cotton bud, and Dad says leave him alone cuz it's not gonna matter about his baby teeth now is it?

There's a pack of Strawberry Bubblicious wedged between the dashboard and the windshield. One square left and it's gone soft and sticky, but I peel off the pink paper and give it to Marty telling him to chew and don't swallow or he's gonna be blowing bubbles out his ass every time he farts and that's a fact.

So I turn the key and crank her into gear and the tires crunch over gravel. I take the driveway nice and easy before wheeling onto the main road. The swallows turn and flash in front of the windshield, and their shadows make Marty blink. I can't look at them too hard; I'm concentrating on keeping the silver wing point on the hood lined up with the road, and scanning the distance for anything coming. But there's nothing except the damn swallows.

Marty spits out his gum, saying he doesn't want it anymore and he's thirsty. I tell him to wait for the lake.

I remembered about the dehydration. I got Dad's old army bag packed with essentials and it sits between us. Two cans from the pop shop, Purple Berry Blitz for Marty and a root beer for me, but I don't know if he'll drink it cuz even his favourite things make him puke now. And I got the bird book cuz I remember Marty likes the pictures, especially the woodpecker with its cartoon-red cone head and crazy eye. Yeah, Marty would laugh at the *tock tock tock* of the bird slamming its head against a tree, and he'd throw himself at me with his hand a jabbing beak and his mouth sputtering and spitting until even Mom told him to stop. And I took it too far as usual.

"Hey Marty," I'd say, "you like peckers, right?"

Right. His eyes wide and trusting and hanging on me.

"Guess that makes you a pecker-head, eh? Say it, Marty, say 'I'm a pecker-head'."

And he would, sputtering *peckerhead peckerhead* and putting on a real show cuz he likes it when I laugh and he's too little and dumb to know anything else.

The swallows turn and my stomach twists and I wonder why it's him got sick not me. But nothing's like it's supposed to be, nothing's legit.

Mom and Dad did what they were supposed to. They took Marty to the hospital when they found the little purple lumps on his legs just before Easter, and they told the doctor about the headaches and the bruises and the fevers. And the hospital did the legit; the tests came out and Marty went in and cried cuz he was missing the first grader's egg hunt, and Mom cried cuz his hair fell out, and Dad and me just stood there looking stupid.

We come to the hill before the lake and I do what Dad always does while we scream laughter and Mom screams stop: I push my foot to the pedal and hold. I gun that gas 'til we're over the peak, 'til we're airborne we're flying we're goddamn birds, and for a moment I forget.

Then the road rears up and we come down and Marty gasps when we bump, like it hurts his bones.

"Sheeit, Marty," I say real quick, "that was a good one. *Wheee.*"

And Marty whispers *wheee* back and smiles and it's okay.

The lake's not much of a lake really. A marshy oval in the neighbour's field, where we come to swim in the early summer, before they let the cows in to graze and the shore turns to shit. Now the water's blue and pure.

I let the Chevy roll to a stop and tell Marty to wait, I'll help him, but he pushes against the door and slides himself out and stands with his knees knobbly bent and his blanket falling. He takes a few steps and I see his shoelace has already come undone and how the hell he's managed that I don't know, but he lets me pick him up and piggyback him to the lake.

I find a log and a dry belt of sand, and wrap Marty in his blanket before wedging him between my knees. I take off his hat so he can feel the summer on his skin, but then I put it back on again cuz his scalp looks so eggshell bare. The sun glazes the water all shimmer and split, and we watch the teal ducks bob and the dragonflies lift. Marty's head leans against my knee and I get a floaty feeling like swimming, even though we're not.

They show up in a swoop of shadow, like swallows but bigger and darker and falling faster. Their wing points turn and dive, flashing between dull black and glorious purple depending on how the light strikes.

"Hey look, Marty," I say. He lifts his head and settles himself back against my chest.

We sit quiet with our eyes following the sharp flight. Marty wants to know if they're woodpeckers and I tell him *naw*, but I have to look them up in the bird book just the same.

"*Sheeit*, Marty," I say, "Purple Martin, an Agile Aerial Acrobat. Must have named it after you, right?"

He smiles and coughs, and I remember the cans of pop in the army bag. I flip the tab off Marty's Purple Berry Blitz and he drinks a little and it almost feels like any summer day at the lake. So we're sitting there watching the birds and I'm thinking nothing and Marty opens his mouth and croaks out a few words.

"You say something, bud?"

"I'm gonna be a bird," he says. "I'm gonna be a bird when I die."

And I can't think what to say and I'm glad he's facing the lake and can't see my face. Then he asks how I'll know him. When he's a bird.

I blink and my eyes clear and I see his foot poking out from under the blanket with its shoelaces trailing.

"I'll know you cuz you'll still be Marty," I say. "Purple Martin. You're gonna be up there feet dragging and falling over yourself, and it won't matter shit when you're a bird.

Yeah, I'll know you."

He leans against me and I can feel his shoulders wing-bone sharp. I know he's getting cold and it's time to go. He doesn't want to leave so I tell him to watch and I put my thumb over his pop can and shake it up real good, until the spray arcs purple and glimmering against the sun and we laugh at the fizzy fart sound it makes.

Marty sleeps on the way back and I take the road slow cuz his head's too knobbly to knock against the window.

Of course Mom and Dad are already home by the time I roll the Chevy up the driveway, cuz nothing's the way it's supposed to be and nothing's legit. Marty wakes when I say sheeit but he smiles and it's okay then.

Dad doesn't say nothing. He bundles Marty out of the car and into the house while I stare at my feet, and Mom comes tearing out of the front door screaming "What the hell got into you?" while her hands flap and smack. She grabs onto my shoulders and her face crumples, like Marty's used to when I was mean, and I hug her, even though I sting where I got slapped.

They ground me for the rest of the summer, but of course I go the funeral and no one remembers to punish me when we get back so I ride my bike to the lake. I take a root beer for me and a Purple Berry Blitz for Marty. It fizzes when I pour it out onto the marshy ground and if the tears come I don't know it cuz now I'm looking up. Watching.

SWEET THE STING

"YOU CAME."

My sister says this through cracked lips, and it isn't a question. It never is. The oxygen hums and the IV drips from pouch to vein. Her sallow hand clutches for mine.

"You gonna save me again?"

There's a trace of the lopsided smile, the one that cuts through the anger with its little girl need. I stay silent because I won't make it easy this time. I know her too well. "You remember that summer," she says, "the wasp nest?" So she knows me even better.

It was one of those hot August days that sticks to the skin and prickles the temper, that forces the cattle under the shade of the paper birches. I'd been sent to muck out the barn.

Amy was meant to be helping but she was five years younger and wearing her ballet costume. The white gauze floated while she tripped from hay bale to bale. "Ring around the rosies," she sang, "pocket full of ponies."

"Posies," I muttered.

Amy ignored me. She tiptoed her way along a shaft of light, her bony arms held out pretty and precarious, her bare feet delicately arched. The wasps droned from the eaves, and my big hands heaved while my toes sweated and slid inside rubber. *"Husha,"* Amy looked at me with wide blue eyes and a little smile as she slipped out the door.

I shovelled another load of manure into the wheelbarrow and cursed her.

Amy had allergies and asthma and rashes; she was born six weeks too soon after a series of alarms. A near loss, said Mom, and all the more precious for it. *And me?* I wanted to ask, but never did. I knew I was the lucky one. I was built like the broad side of a barn and never a worry.

"Husha," came Amy's voice from outside the door.

I swatted away a wasp. It had been a bad year for yellowjackets.

We found their papery nests in every shelter: under the eaves, clinging to fence posts and tree branches, and even once in the front seat of the old Ford. Dad sprayed the nests at dusk when the wasps had gone drowsy. Amy and I stood on the porch in our nightgowns to watch, balancing on our tiptoes and holding our breath. She giggled as the first bodies circled and fell like drunks in a stupor and I told her to shush, but Dad stopped anyway. "You let her come this close?" he said. "You're supposed to be the older one. Use your goddamn head." So I grabbed Amy by a hand sticky with thumb-sucking and hauled her upstairs to bed. "Deb," she said, her arms reaching for me. "Deb, I wasn't scared. You were there." *"Husha husha,"* sang Amy now, and I could hear her feet crackling over dry grass.

My toes sweated and the wasps buzzed and bumped against the beams above. Husha. There was a thud as Amy jumped onto the old log just outside the barn door, the one Dad kept saying he'd cut up for firewood, but never did because Amy cried. She needed the log, needed it for a princess path and a ballerina stage and fashion model runway; she needed it because she was going be a star. *Husha husha.* I let my shovel clatter against the floor and rubbed my neck. My hands hurt and my head ached and my sister hummed and bounced.

"We all fall down," I hollered. Mean. Some part of me seeing her tumble onto her frilly ass. Willing it even.

Silence. My head buzzed high and tight, and the wasps circled.

"We all fall *down*," sang Amy. High and pure, making it sound goddamn great, like something we'd all want given the choice. Another thud, softer this time.

Then she screamed. Sharp enough to break skin, high and hurt and spiralling down to just one sound repeated. *Deb deb deb.*

I came running.

The heat slammed into me, and the sunlight stung my eyes after the dark of the barn. I blinked. Amy flailed and flapped, one foot stuck up to the ankle in the log and the other hopping, screaming so loud my ears fizzed. Her gauze skirt floated up, and out swirled a cloud of shadow. I blinked again and the shadow disintegrated. It landed on me like hissing rain, feather-light but sticking to skin, and the pain came a split second and a thousand needles later and I yelped and danced, I stumbled towards Amy and lifted her up and away while the air roared around us. The wasps fell like a rain of hot needles and Amy screamed and screamed while

I brushed and slapped and bolted, all the way to the front door where Mom stood with a dishtowel in her hands and her mouth open.

"What?" she said, "Deb? What, how could you . . . ?"

Then she was on the move, hauling us inside and slamming the door, her towel slapping and her foot stomping while the furious little bodies pulsed against the linoleum. I stood shivering with Amy boneless and wheezing against me. *Deb deb deb.*

"Deb," Mom pushed at me, "get her to the truck." She scrambled for the keys.

We ran outside with the wasps still buzzing, and then I was in the passenger seat with Amy propped over my lap and Mom lurching the pickup onto the road.

"Push her head back," yelled Mom, "keep her airway open."

I shifted Amy over my knees until her head tilted backwards and her mouth gaped. Her skin was hot and it burned where her body touched mine, but I held her tight, even while my hands slipped with sweat and my gut pitched and my head buzzed black and yellow.

"Deb deb deb," Amy bubbled, her eyelids swelling and her breath rasping. She turned her head and puked up milky white against my rubber boots. Stripes wavered in front of my eyes.

"Ring around the rosies," I whispered, "pocket full of ponies." She sucked in air and a triangle hollowed between her collarbones. "*Husha husha,*" I pleaded. A little smile before she puked again and her breath came out a shrill whistle.

Amy was barely breathing by the time we got to the hospital. The nurses gathered her up in a flurry of white, and Mom clung to the stretcher and left me. I stood for a time with my hands hanging. My rubber boots hummed with sour stink and the receptionist told me to sit down.

I counted my stings as the minutes passed. Twelve, thirteen. Perfect red circles and hardly any swelling. I pulled off my boots and slid them under my chair, and a few smashed corpses fell from my feet. Nineteen, twenty. The receptionist looked at me then went back to her magazine.

Amy could die. I tasted this thought. No more wide blue eyes, no more good night kisses and gummy-sweet hand. My throat burned and my eyes blurred and I counted my stings until I got to twenty-three and had to start again. Amy could die and we would bury her in the ground. I would wear something black and gauzy, I'd lift my veil so they could all see my tears and know that I was suffering too. Amy could die and I would be the one watched for the near loss and more precious for it.

But Amy didn't die. My parents took turns sitting with her and I was left home with a list of chores. If my thoughts came back to me in a gut-twist of shame, I would shovel harder and hose down the troughs a little longer, I would work until my palms blistered and the sweat ran into my eyes. The wasps circled and buzzed, and I swatted at them with my bare hands, willing them to sting me. They did not. Their high thin hum filled my head when I sat at the dinner table with whatever parent was home that night, silent and white with exhaustion. *Please please please*, I'd catch myself thinking, with no idea of what I was hoping for.

Amy was in the hospital for a couple of weeks. When she came home, Dad doused the ballerina stage with gasoline and Amy and I roasted marshmallows over its remains. Amy wanted to hold her own stick and cried when she got melted goo in her ponytail, and Mom asked how could I, with Amy's hair baby-fine and her hands still bandaged.

Amy danced on a real stage after that. The years passed in ballet white and princess pink and homecoming blue, and I scrubbed my big hands with pumice so I could clap through her curtsies. The attention Amy got didn't bother me. I had it figured out by then. I was big-boned and practical around the farm and I knew Dad was grateful I'd turned down college and the neighbour's son and the backpacking trip around Europe with my friends. I was needed. But sometimes the autumn wind would come through paper birches and set their heart-shaped leaves to trembling, and I would feel something stab at me, something as stark as the stripes of peeling bark and as sorrowful as those yellow leaves falling.

I stayed and Amy left. Amy was beyond us, beyond a barn and some cows, beyond dance lessons in the school gym and recitals on a church hall stage. My parents sold the far field to the neighbour's son and pooled the milk money, and it was enough to send Amy to the School of Performing Arts. The local newspaper did an article. It was official; Amy was going to be a star.

The seasons came and went, the years marked in variations of heat and rain, in volumes of hay and milk and shit to be shovelled. I took pride from the silver canisters filled and waiting, I took peace from the summer dusk falling.

Amy sent us long letters at first, then the occasional photo or clipping from a magazine. She was thin and glossy and unrecognisable. When she phoned, she bubbled and chirped at the other end — this party, these people, we wouldn't believe who'd been there and what they'd done. Dad would pass it around the feed store later and get all the names wrong.

Amy did visit. She arrived in denim and cowboy boots, but her jeans were cut close to her body and her toecaps free of dirt. With her face scrubbed clean, she looked something like the sister I remembered. But the edginess at the dinner table was new; she picked up her fork and put it down again, she spoke in exclamations and ate in little bursts. She followed me out to the barn after I did the dishes, and sparked up a joint.

"Oh Jesus," she said when I gave her a look, "you would not believe, Deb, you just would not *believe*."

She was eighteen. I was five years older and didn't know what I could tell her.

I drove her home from the city the year she played the nurse in a hospital drama. She needed every gas station restroom, and told me it was a bladder infection while she swiped at her nose.

The snow cancelled her return flight the next Christmas, and she curled up in bed for three days of retching and moaning. She told my parents it was stomach flu.

Dad thought it was that, the same stomach flu, which kept him in bed for the rest of the winter. By the time he was diagnosed, Amy had landed the lead in a romantic comedy. The theatre sold out of tickets when the movie came to our town, but Dad watched the trailer on the hospital television. "That guy she's with?" he said. "What's his name? How come she never brought him home? Why is she so *skinny* now?" Another time he refused to look at the magazines I brought. "That's not her. Where is she? Did you girls have words, did you do something, Deb?" I could understand his confusion. Amy on film looked like somebody else, from somewhere else. She didn't belong to people like us now.

Amy came to Dad's funeral in dark glasses and a heavy coat she kept on after the sun came out. I told Mom it was the grief, guessing at the marks under the long sleeves.

Amy made the cover of Vogue that year. The local newspaper ran the story and a reporter called for a comment. I flipped through the farm equipment catalogue and said we were proud, so very proud, and could they send us a copy because Mom framed all of Amy's clippings on her memory wall.

I told Mom it was man trouble when Amy didn't call for a year. Man trouble was believable for someone who looked like Amy. And Mom believed me when I said I'd been talking to the neighbour's son on the subject of goats, and he'd highly recommended the livestock exhibition held in the city.

"You go," she said. "Maybe you could look up Amy while you're there. Just to make sure she's okay."

Amy's condo smelled worse than any goat shed. I washed the dishes and paid the bills and got Amy into a clinic. I rubbed her back when she sobbed, and I nodded when she told me she would never let it happen again, not again, not ever ever. I stayed until she stopped picking at her scabs and could nibble toast without retching.

I told Mom that Amy was fine and goats were too much trouble; they got into everything and were helpless against predators.

There was no one to tell after Mom died. No one to tell after the service, with the old aunties fogged with punch and their men bound in suits, and the neighbour's son asking what I'd do now with no one to care for. There was no one to tell when Amy appeared in the supermarket tabloids and the auditions dried up and she called to whisper for money.

Once I answered the phone to a line gone dead and thought I heard my name in the hum. Deb deb deb.

Amy sat in the hospital garden after that one. She told me to let her go, that I'd always hated her anyway.

I should have said something but the bees buzzed in the roses and I think their hum soothed me to silence.

Husha husha.

"Why do you always come?" Amy mumbled.

I had no answer to that.

Six weeks later she overdosed again.

❦

The oxygen hums and the IV drips and I hold my big hands together.

"You remember that summer?" Amy asks. "You remember the wasp nest?"

"Of course," I say, reaching for her hand. "I nearly lost you."

"Those stings hurt," Her cracked lips try a smile. "But you know something, Deb? I was high with it too, the falling down and you there to catch me."

The oxygen hums and I stay quiet.

"God, how do you stand it," she says. Her eyes drift shut.

It's been a bad year for yellowjackets. I look for the drift and cloud of them, listen for the low roar that betrays the nest. I wait for evening to aim the nozzle at the dark opening and pull the trigger. The wasps swarm and drop, and I see Amy tripping from hay bale to bale with her white gauze floating and her arms held out delicately, and I know she'll always need me. That I'm always there, that I'll hold onto an empty line just to hear my name.

I look for the wasp nests in every shelter, and I spray them when the dusk comes.

MARRAKECH

"MARRAKECH," MY MOTHER WOULD SAY, "Marrakech was somewhere else."

She'd peel off my snow-damp socks and drape them over the back of a chair in front of the woodstove. They'd steam silently, and everything I hated about my childhood was there in that musty odour of wool.

"In Marrakech, the sun beat down hot and the air smelled medieval," my mother would say as I stretched out my legs, watching my waxy toes redden. "Oh Aisha, the perfumes of the medina! Cumin and coriander, and attar of rose. Cinnamon sticks and seed pods of cardamom, and the turmeric a dry shocking gold. The souk vendors would pile them up in pyramids of colour, and their little burners blazed day and night with benzoin. And the old plague doctors, they'd fasten little pouches of aromatics around their necks and fashion beaks of posies for their noses, to drive away the smell of sickness. Those spices, they're strong enough to cover the stench of the dead. Can you imagine that, Aisha? Every bad thing, every rotten memory, carried off on a drift of petal."

Then her eyes would stray, darting from the scarves flung over our second-hand sofa to the intricately patterned rugs that hid the worst of the peeling lino. The colours jangled my eyes but not so my mother; it was the mention of Marrakech that made her restless. She'd spring up to open a window despite the cold outside, and her hands would flutter and float until they found her basket of yarns.

"The rugs were so well woven," she'd say, her hands calming over the clacking needles, "Perfectly patterned, balanced and geometric. Nothing real, Aisha, no people allowed in those rugs."

Our home was filled with her knitting. She had her own sense of colour, my mother, with shades grouped according to what she would call spiritual semantics rather than conventional aesthetics. It was a question of balance, she told me, Yin and Yang. Saffron needed its fiery nature calmed with imperial purple, wild lime was tamed by sludge brown, while rusty earth could only be coupled with deep turquoise. All these hues worked out their issues on our living room cushions. My mother drifted into my bedroom to paint my walls sky blue and knit my bedspread shades of orange. She would have me sleep with the setting sun. Every night, she'd wrench open a window and instruct the whistling wind to blow the bad dreams away and keep me safe.

We lived in the kind of apartment block favoured by retirees and welfare cases, and it was obvious which ones we were. I was a quiet child, and this earned me some illicit sugary treats at a few dinette suites around the building. The furniture there was always coffee-coloured and the wallpaper a floral beige and, more often than not, I had to sit on a step stool for the lack of chairs. I was sometimes invited to a classmate's birthday party or Saturday sleepover and from this I learned that other children lived in whole houses. You took off your shoes at the door so you did not mark the pale squishy carpet that ran up the steps and into all the rooms. You did not bounce on the squeaky leather sofa, or run your hands over the shiny surfaces or touch the sharp-edged ornaments on the shelves. But it was the mothers of other children that most astounded me. These mothers came home from work with their hair pinned up over big shouldered suits and their lips glossed crimson. They'd smile tiredly and kick off pointy pumps to rub their toes, telling us to eat our potato chips at the kitchen bar. All that shine was awful for showing the grease.

Our apartment was not shiny. It was frequently hazy with smoke from the cigarettes my mom smoked, or from the incense she lit to hide the ashtray smell. My mother wore squat sandals with woolly socks and kept her shoes on in the house. I would ask her why she did not wear black suits like the other mothers, or go to work in high-heeled pumps. I kept my eyes wide and my voice sweet, but I knew what I was doing. My mother's would flutter and reach for another cigarette, and my gut would twist.

"Marrakech," she'd say, "In Marrakech we all wore little slippers and shuffled the streets, slow in the heat of the sun. Oh Aisha, those little slippers! Some of them satin and embroidered with flowers, some of them fastened with silver bells. Like harem girls we were, padding soft and silent around the sleeping sultan."

I wore whatever shoes my mother could find at the second-hand store. Scuffed patent Mary Janes one year, a pair of clunky oxfords the next. The gym teacher would not let me take PE lessons without white sneakers, and sent increasingly strident letters home advising my mother of the school rules. My mother would fold and tear these notes, skewering the quarters to the nail protruding from kitchen wall. They would join the reminders of appropriate school dress, and the overdue library notices and electricity bills. I was instructed not to open our door should anyone come knocking. I hid the notes my mother sent back to my teachers; I could not bear the brown butcher's paper they were written on.

I'd pick sly holes in my mother's knitting out of spite. My mother would say nothing while her hands unravelled the wool to start over again. Peg's Yarn Barn had agreed to take some pieces, after my mother had read the owner's tarot over a cup of rosehip tea. Peg is a woman soon to be blessed, my mother told me, in both fortune and love. I thought this unlikely, as Peg was ancient and smelled of cat pee, and always seemed to give us too much change back. Nevertheless, my mother's sweaters and scarves glared out their dissonances from the dimmest corner of the store from then on. My mother would drag me there at the end of every month and sometimes Peg would smile and hand us an envelope of money. More often, we would leave with our arms piled high with the unsold merchandise, the gaudy colours amplifying my shame.

I would have to wear the worst of it. No point in spending money when we had perfectly good clothes in our hands, my mother would announce, and look at the spice market shades of this or the desert sun in that; surely this is the antidote to all the rain we've been having lately? My hatred would spike pure and hot, and blacker than any storm cloud.

I hated it too, when the cold came. I knew I would have to hurry out the school gates, my bare arms freezing, until I reached the cover of the pines just before the apartment block. A quick rummage in my backpack and the sweater would be over my head, with the clashing hat pulled low over my face. Then it was just a short slink through the side street and I would be safely home.

Sometimes I was caught out. Someone would eventually point out the beany smell of my packed lunch or the lack of parent on open afternoon. It might be a substitute teacher trying to pronounce my name to the delight of my class-mates, or a girl in the company of other girls, each with a sing-song voice and a head tilted in concern. I would come home drenched in drizzle and bristling with humiliation. My mother would peel off my rainbow colours and run me a bath.

"Aisha, did I tell you," my mother would ask, her hands aflutter, "Did I tell you about the Hamman, the public baths?"

It didn't matter if she had. I could dunk my head, block my ears with bathwater, and still she would talk.

"Picture us then, a line of women making our way there in the afternoon. We'd enter the steamy room one by one to wait our turn, we'd stand there naked in all our ages but unashamed. This was another country, Aisha, and the usual rules of propriety did not apply.

They'd float petals in the water for us and the smell of roses and jasmine made my head drift. The bravest went first into that scalding hot water and the frailest waited until it had become tepid and cloudy. They'd scrub us down with rough loofahs, and they were not gentle with it, but how clean you were after! How floaty free you felt! Darling, you will take the Hammam with me some day."

I'd ask where the men were, my eyes averted.

"The men? Ah the men. We never saw them; they went to the baths in the morning."

Sometimes I would wonder aloud about my father, about why there was no father in our home. I was crafty; I'd let the question drift out like an afterthought. My mother would change the subject. She would tell me about Marrakech.

"Did I tell you, Aisha," she'd say, "Did I tell you that I had an admirer there?"

She'd met him at the medina. His dark eyes followed her as she wandered, as she pointed and mimed at the exotic fruits, as she laughed when they did not understand her garbled attempts at their dialect. The men brushed past, sometimes lingering a little too long and a little too close. One of them smiled and made reassuring sounds while he tried to force her into a narrow close. Her admirer rescued her, and he became both her interpreter and her protector.

"We took mint tea in the café." My mother would smile and look almost pretty. "He asked me question after question in that odd English of his, his hands stilled and waiting. His dark eyes never left mine when I spoke. I had his undivided attention and sometimes I fear it went to my head, for I would tell him the most fantastic stories. He would ponder whatever I said with the same sobriety. He had a bald head and he was not young but it didn't matter, he was by far the best listener I had ever known. Soon I was in love with him."

"What happened next?" I'd ask grudgingly, taken in again.

"Ah well," sighed my mother, "Good listeners are few and far between, and that quality is particularly rare in a man. I had a rival, another western lady much like myself but blonder and with eyes a deeper shade of blue. She connived and lied; she worked her manipulations and soon my lover and I were separated. I saw him again, some time after, but his hands would not rest. They played with his spoon, they stirred the sugar into his tea, and round and round they went. I talked, and his eyes strayed from mine and to his hands, to the little whirlpool they made. I knew then. I knew I had lost him. I could not abide the smell of mint after, Aisha."

She could tell a story, my mother. I would almost forgive her the gauzy skirts and circus colours, the frizzed and hennaed hair that made her look like a clown. I could almost forget the atrocities of my hand-knitted childhood. But I was getting older, and so were the kids from school. I dreaded being seen with her in town.

"Hippie," they'd snigger, and mime the smoking of a joint. "Hey man, where'd I leave my weed?"

My mother never touched drugs that I knew, not even painkillers or penicillin. She distrusted doctors and modern medicine. My colds were treated with salt water gargles and teaspoons of honey, my rashes and pimples with rosewater. Later, I snuck out to the parties in those clean modern houses and I was passed acrid smelling pipes and little neon patches of paper. I saw how the girls glanced sideways at each other, then at me, and I knew I wasn't one of them no matter what I did. I saw how the boys circled, both casual and insistent, and I knew I wasn't safe. I stopped going to parties. I worked hard at school instead and I got a scholarship to go to university.

I studied sociology and learned we were disadvantaged; I studied history and learned we were the remnants of a counter culture. I studied cynicism and finally understood that the difference between rich hippies and real ones was the cut of their clothes and the duration of their delusions. I came home for the holidays and talked to my mother.

"What happened?" I asked, "Between Marrakech and this, what happened?

"Oh darling," she said, "Life. Life happened."

She was working part-time in the new age shop then. She dressed in all the colours of her aura and told the customers about crystals. Her hand-knit things still lurked in the back, and sometimes they sold for prices that almost justified their cacophony. The nineties had arrived with their promise of gentler times, and our way of life was nearly mainstream by then. The university students did yoga and hung tie-dyed scarves on their walls. They'd rediscovered patchouli and mismatched woollens, and suddenly it was hip to punch holes in tins and use them for candle-holders. The dorms looked like versions of my childhood home, albeit newer and more deliberate. My mother was oblivious to the changes. She got an employee's discount on sticks of sandalwood and she was happy.

I wore black and changed my major. I studied economics and learned that my mother was insignificant. My mother had drifted free of the system, she had made little contribution to labour, she did not bank or borrow, and she had neither savings nor pension. She had drifted free and she was not safe.

I went to work in a bank. I bought a pair of glossy red pumps with my first paycheque and took out an investment portfolio with my second. A percentage of my earnings appeared on the cheque I sent my mother every month. I bought a glossy red car to go with the pumps and I was happy. I worked hard, I spent money, I aspired to the same things as everyone else. I bought a condo and furnished it with leather sofas and pointy ornaments in neutral shades. I thought I was safe.

I attracted my own admirers. I would reheat things from the better shops in my gleaming chrome kitchen and, after a glass or two of deep red wine, I would tell stories about my mother. Her ghastly colours and the hand-knitted horrors, her insistence on an open window despite the weather. I was good with the descriptions and my admirer would gaze at me, rapt. The punchline was always Marrakech and he'd laugh accordingly. I could smile too, I could afford to be a bit of a character now that I was safe.

If my guts twinged, if I remembered how my mother's hands could flutter when I hurt her, I reminded myself of that monthly payment. It wasn't as though I didn't talk to her. I phoned every month and she told me about the colours she'd knit into her newest project, or how the man with the bad stomach had benefitted from the application of tourmaline. It wasn't as though I didn't listen. I'd tell her I was glad she was keeping busy, while I flipped through my accounts and answered my emails.

She began to talk about Marrakech again, about how she would go back one day. I didn't hear any change in her voice. I could not hear the cells mutating and multiplying but I think she could.

The call came late one Tuesday, and I arranged a week off work. The hospital stank the way hospitals do, with the sickly sweet odour of urine layered between bleach and some kind of floral disinfectant. My mother lay with bright hair frizzed round her, like a pale stemmed rose between the sheets.

The doctors said it was advanced, and there would be little time.

"These doctors, you know I never liked them much," said my mother from between parched lips. I pressed for more; I hated that these might be her last words.

"Marrakech," I said, "Tell me about the medina, the souk. Tell me about your admirer."

"Marrakech," said my mother, "It was somewhere else, Aisha. It smelled of cinnamon and roses, of benzoin burning."

They asked what I wanted done after, and I thought of our apartment, of every window open even in winter, of my mother's fear of being shut in. I thought of ashes on the wind and chose cremation.

My mother had kept things over the years. I found a bundle of unopened letters in her dresser drawer.

My aunt was willing to meet with me. She sits across from me at my kitchen table now and her eyes are very blue.

She smokes and I don't stop her. I can smell something of my mother in that dusty sweet odour.

"Ah, your mother," she says, "She was always an odd one. Off in her own world, you know? The stories she told! As good as real, with all the colours and smells so clear you could almost see it in front of you. She might have made movies or written books if it weren't for the breakdown. Different days back then . . . you acted strange and you were noticed. Strange got you taken away pretty damn quick."

I didn't think it sounded all that different from now, but I keep my mouth shut.

"Your mother spent time in the hospital," my aunt says, "Mental hospital, I mean. Went to visit her and was appalled. The stink of the place, that got you first; then that sickly pale green everywhere. Her doctor was a total creep. Sucked on breath mints and stared at you. Bald old bastard. Couldn't keep his hand out of the cookie jar, I heard, especially with the young and pretty ones." She takes another drag on her cigarette. "Now the last straw was the baths. You wouldn't believe it, it was like something from the Middle Ages. They lined up all the women naked as jaybirds, no dignity or respect, and made them wait their turn. They ran the water so hot that the first in would be scalded, they scrubbed so hard they drew blood. I saw that and I knew I had to get your mother out. So. I argued, I lied, I sweet-talked that baldy doctor and finally I threatened. He caved in; he knew I had his number." She exhales and it sounds like a sigh. "Your mother never forgave me. I think she was sweet on the creep, he'd done some of that mind control on her, you know? They had places for people just out of hospital back then and your mother lived in one of those for a while. Run by hippies. She had to leave after she had you; they didn't allow kids. Jesus, I never even knew she was pregnant. I wrote at Christmas, I sent a card on her birthday, but she never wrote back."

My auntie stubs out her cigarette and looks at me. Her eyes are a bluer version of my mother's, and her hair might have been blonde once. I don't ask about Marrakech. I can guess how her eyes will cloud in confusion and how her mouth will form the denial.

I will open the window once she leaves, then I will sit down at my computer. A flight will be easy enough to find; it's popular holiday destination for those looking to escape the winter rain. I will not take my red pumps or my grey suits. This is another country and the usual rules of propriety will not apply. I'll buy the gauziest of skirts at the souk; I'll clash my colours freely and shuffle the streets in squat sandals.

I'll go with my mother of course. I think of her carried like a little pouch of aromatics around the neck, and I smile. I think she will forgive me the aesthetics for the semantics. We will wallow in the perfumes of the medina and our memories will unravel like bad knitting. We will drench ourselves in the rainbow hues of the souk and be safe. We will take the Hammam and we will float free as rose petals scattered. I'll go with my mother and we will be somewhere else together.

THE LAKE OF BONES

STACI TELLS ME IN THE KITCHEN when we hardly got any time at all, maybe twenty minutes, maybe half an hour before her auntie gets back. She's wearing her skinny jeans and stands bent over the sink, running water into the kettle. We got this thing going; she pretends to make me tea and I pretend that I'm going to drink it. She's so sweet and curved standing there that my hands find her hips and I press against her, not thinking anything much except that we got twenty minutes.

Oh God, she says. Would you just stop.

And I lean back a bit. She calls the shots and I'm okay with that. Most times.

She pulls away from me and puts the kettle on the stove. Oh my God, she says again and pushes her hair back from her face.

I see the bruised look under her eyes, the cluster of little spots next to her mouth. And I think maybe it's her auntie, maybe it's the cancer come back.

When she tells me she's late I don't feel anything at all. I say the first thing that comes to mind, which is that she's still got time to do something about it. That I got money and I can pay.

LOST BOYS

The Lake of Bones is what I think about when she kicks me out. And I get this crazy idea; if I could take her there, if I could find the bones, everything would work itself out. Everything would be okay. If we could go back again.

❦

The Lake of Bones is something we all know. We know it if we're Carrier or Chilcotin or some kind of white, if we're reserve or ranch or if we got one of those fancy apartments in town. It's part of being from here, like the sweathouse and the shot-up road signs and the pack of horses left to run wild down the stampede grounds. The Lake of Bones is handed to us by the old men on the salmon run, mouthed around a bottle of Jack like they don't want the women to hear. The Lake of Bones gets told in skookum accents by the brush-cut white boys, at the Bible camp where we all went on account of it being free and the food not too bad, and not because we were any kind of Christian. The Lake of Bones is passed around a crouched circle with a joint, taking on a sparkle with every telling, glittering like broken glass in the playground after dark. Yeah, we'd go to the Lake with this girl or that one. We'd take them there and they'd be so freaked they'd let us do anything we wanted. The Lake of Bones is a terrible thing, terrible because of what's underneath and hidden, but it's a comfort too. It's something that belongs to us.

My Grandfather told me. He said, "Listen, hey boy you listen, this is for you. But don't listen too hard to the words. You got to see what's there, even if you go to the lake and don't see nothing at all.

The Lake of Bones

There's no people in Grandfather's story. It happened before the people came, when the elk were still here.

It's winter in this story, late winter, and the days are shifting between crackling cold and watery sunlight. Sometimes there's a smell of sap in the air. There's nothing to eat; it's too early for that. The Elk People step through the brittle birches, steaming and snorting, stopping to gnaw at lichen, and hoof at the crusted snow. They're padded with winter fur but underneath that, the rib and hip and spine bones poke. There are many of them and each is bound to the other, and in each acid-pool eye there's a long history of grandmothers and sisters and aunties, in each throat a song of names. This is the time before the people, when the animals had voices.

The winter night comes early and each morning there are fewer of the Elk People. The wolves and coyotes and ravens follow by day, and when the moon rises, their eyes flash silver. Grandfather and Grandmother Elk look around and see their people are starving. They head south. When they come to end of the forest, there's a lake, a lake so huge the treeline is a fringe of lashes around an unblinking eye. The winter sunlight warms their backs and the ice creaks and shifts underneath their hooves, singing a water song under its breath. Grandmother stops and Grandfather looks back at the wolves flickering between the birches. The Elk People step onto the ice.

At first it seems that everything will work out, that everything will be okay. The ice creaks and shudders, but it holds. The herd steps out, hoofing and snorting, breathing in like the wind will hold them.

The ice breaks near the middle of the lake. It happens fast; the surface juddering and pitching, black fissures snaking underneath, the sheets buckling up and over each other. The entire herd goes through.

How long it takes, who can say? There are no people in this story. There's no time. At some point, the water stops churning and the wolves loop back through the birches. The ravens circle once, twice, before settling. The coyotes sing the moon into the sky.

When the wind stops and the water is calm, when the light is low and your eye unclouded, you can see to the bottom of the lake. Picture this; row upon row of ribcages, leg bones scattered and antlers reaching, skulls turned over like empty cups. When the light is right, you can see those bones. But I never have. And every time someone tells the story, I think of my Grandfather wiping his mouth and lifting his chin, staring at me like he knows something I don't, something the story doesn't tell. I think of my little sister swearing there's a burial ground for horses under the school playing field, or the camp counsellors and their Jesus dead and rising, or my old science teacher describing the cat in a box. Same look, same tone of voice, every time. We got something you don't.

The Lake of Bones was where I took Staci the first time we hooked up. But she wasn't one of those girls. It wasn't like that. The lake was always so pretty in late spring. I had Grandfather's canoe and I knew the quiet places where we could paddle, away from the drinking parties and make-out couples. I had a good job and a mobile home on an acre of land off the rez. I could drink legal and pay for it too.

But when Staci climbed into my pickup truck and wedged her book bag between her knees and looked at me, I could hardly breathe. Staci is the kind of girl who can speak long strings of French and balance equations, who can connect each war to the other and draw the inside of a lily. Staci is the kind of girl who rocked her last year of high school while I sat behind her, red-eyed and smirking. She's taking a few courses at the community college and planning to go to university, and she says I should come, maybe try for some kind of trades bursary off Indian Affairs. And I say yeah, maybe I should. But the mill pays good and steady, and the only thing I use my status card for is cheap gas and ciggies at the reserve Stop'n'Go. I don't even look Indian, no more than she does anyway.

So I sit in my truck, flipping through my playlist, thinking of putting on something old and classic and true, something my dad might've listened to if he'd stuck around. Springsteen, John Cougar Mellencamp. But I don't have anything like that.

The truck rocks and shifts when Staci gets in. I turn down my music. She hates the boom bass, says the words are disrespectful to women.

You need to listen to me, she says.

Okay, I say.

She begins to cry and pokes around in the glove compartment for the paper towel. I start the engine and wait. But then she wipes her eyes with her fists and looks straight ahead so I drive us to the Lake.

It's early in the season and no one else is there. We find the canoe under the willows where we'd left it last summer.

I brush out the leaves and check for packrats and snakes. Staci takes off her sneakers and places them side by side on the shore, then guides the bow into the lake. It's so quiet I can hear her breath, the glide of water against her calves, a hermit thrush wavering somewhere above us. There's no wind and the water is glassy and full of sky.

I stroke out and Staci sits with her back to me, paddling in time, steady and sure and not needing to look. I don't know where we're going except away from shore, towards the middle of the lake. I figure she'll talk when she's ready.

In the end it's me that stops. My arm muscles are fine, toughened up by the lumber lot, but the shore is a long ways away on every side. I think of the water, the cold of it, the black weight closing overhead, and I put down my paddle. Staci shifts around.

My auntie has the summer cabin, she says. We could fix it up. Make it nice.

Yeah, I say.

This isn't a bad place to raise a kid, she says. You got a job. I could run cash at the Stop'n'Go once the baby's older. Once he's in preschool.

He?

Or she. Whatever. Does it matter? The cabin's big enough and we could do up the inside. Paint it up. Any colour you want, and keep the front room for the baby. Sit at our own kitchen table and drink coffee in the morning, buy a real nice sofa for the living room, maybe leather like the one Jaylen's got, and get one of those big flat screens. We could do up the back bedroom and sleep in our own bed and make as much noise as we want. I can learn to cook. It's not too late to put in a garden, maybe lettuce to start, carrots and peas and beans next year if we plan ahead.

And I can see this, the bed and the sofa and the garden. Staci as she was, her hair tangled and our skin salted together, her face turned against the late light slanting across the lake. Staci as she would be, drowsy on a Sunday morning, arms flung and in no hurry, all the time in world and no worry of her auntie walking in. How this could be.

We could make it our own thing, she says. We could do it different. You're not your dad.

I can see this. I'm not my dad. I would stick around. I can see her and me, making it our own thing. I can see the mill day passing, me coming home and her holding the baby, the dinner in lidded pots and the cutlery in folded napkins just like a magazine, how she'd try so hard to do it right. The days and the days and the days. How this could be.

God. Say something.

I look at her. There's no wind and her hair lies in damp strings around her face. The water is a solid greeny black and I got the feeling the canoe is suspended, that if I was to lean my hand over the side it would bounce off something hard as glass.

Yeah, I say. Maybe.

Oh God, she says. Her fists ball and mash at her eye sockets.

I pick up the paddle. There's a skitter of light on the lake, a fleshy oval dipping and spiralling; a paddle, a face turning away.

You don't love me, she says.

I love you. I'm sure I think the words. But it's freaking me out, all that water beneath us and how far to the bottom you can't even tell.

Staci's crying hard now. I know I'm supposed to do something, to find the right thing to say and make it okay. I stroke over one side, then the other. The water grabs and pulls against the paddle, my arms strain, and for a while this is all I can think about, the push against that flat heavy lake and the need for land.

I love you, I say, when she's shoving into her sneakers.

I love you, I say, as she stumbles up the bank.

And it feels like love, this long deep breath that pushes past my throat and uncurls in my lungs. It feels like love to be on my feet while the ground settles beneath me, like love when the lake closes over the wake we cut through it.

Staci says hello when she's back in town over the holiday breaks. She's usually with her university friends so we don't talk much, just hello how's it going and see you around, yeah? She looks all right. She looks the same.

I got my job at the mill. Sometimes I hook up with one of the girls at Roxy's, depends on the Saturday crowd and what kind of mood I'm in. I don't call them after and they don't expect me to.

Sometimes I go out to the lake. I sit on the overturned canoe with a beer or a joint, doesn't matter what so long as I got something to do with my hands. The water is always that flat green black. The idea that you could ever see to the bottom is someone else's bullshit. I think of the clean white bones, no flesh on them. A thing of beauty once the blood is gone and the sinew stripped. You could pick up those bones and run your hands across them, you could turn them over and over and get no closer to what they mean.

Sometimes when the weed buzzes through my blood, when the wind stills and the light slants across the lake just right, I get a sense of it. The ground shifts under my feet and the water looks solid as glass. How it must have been: the steaming panic, the shock of descent, the crushing weight of water. How it must have been; the last one left on shore and the glitter of eyes between the birches, the creak and pitch of ice ahead. The split second to choose.

WAYLAID BY BEAUTY

LUCE IS THINKING HOW STUPID, how stupid to walk all the way there, in a silk dress and stumbling shoes with the sky bunched for rain (and never mind the sunlight and lark song and how it rolls over the meadow like an exemption), how stupid and how to explain to Simon without looking stupid when out of nowhere the deer clatters across the gravel shoulder and onto the path. It wobbles and splays, then folds at her feet.

Her knees lock. She stares.

It's small, not grown enough for the season. Its fur is spotted with white and its flanks heave under jutting hip bones. She can see the rain beading the eyelashes, and the astonishing marbled blue of the iris. A summer fawn.

"Where's your mommy?" Luce intends a whisper, like you'd use on a sleeping child, but her voice sounds rusty and wrong. Some other woman's voice. Some other woman's words.

The fawn opens its baby mouth and bleats. The sound pitches Luce backwards and her heels spike in the mud.

Has it been hit, was there a car? She didn't hear anything passing. The fawn gazes at her with its marbled eye. Its fur is perfect and unmarked. There's no dragging leg or twisted spine or gash of blood.

It bleats again, raw and hurt.

"Shh," Luce says. "Shush little baby." She crouches and her hand reaches out, hovers, comes to rest on the skinny neck. The fawn lies perfectly still. She strokes down its back, feeling each vertebrae like prayer beads under her fingers. Maybe there's something wrong inside?

Luce sees how this could be. It happens all the time; the bump of metal on flesh, the panicked escape and shudder of internal organs, a slow rupture. You wouldn't know by looking. But maybe it wasn't an accident, maybe there was something wrong from the start. It's so small. Too small for the season.

The fawn closes its eyes. Something wrong and now this. Nature's way.

She should call someone. Who? SPCA, Wildlife Rescue? Simon would know, but Simon is not here. She gets to her feet, wipes her hands on her skirt and fishes around in her bag. No phone. Of course not. It's with her umbrella on the motel room table. She can't even call to say she'll be late, that she decided to walk after a sliver of sun caught her eye and gladdened her, that this feeling was like happiness. She can't call to let Simon know she's trying.

The fawn lies with its chin in the dirt, motionless except for the flanks heaving in and out. The drizzle beads on its fur and the spots are luminous in the grey light. Pretty. Maybe it isn't hurt at all, just stunned. She takes a few steps backwards, scans the field of golden grass, the late summer tansy. Nothing moves.

The mother will come for it. Luce is sure that she's read this somewhere . . . best to leave things be, best to move on. Let nature take its course. The mother will come.

At least it's stopped raining. She takes a tissue from her handbag and dabs it over her face, cheek to cheek, forehead and chin. It's late. She needs to go. Luce leaves the fawn in the dirt and walks on.

A fawn, fallen right at her feet. She'll need to tell Simon. She'll tell him about the marbled blue, the way the eye looked like a tiny galaxy.

❦

He's already there and talking to the waiter, his back to the door and one arm draped over his chair. Casual but arranged, cuffs rolled neatly and nape of neck newly shorn. He must have seen the barber. He must be trying. Luce knows how a haircut changes him, takes him from beautiful to beyond question, bone by sharpened bone. The waiter sees this too; it's there in her wide eyes, the swallow swoop of her smile as she listens to him.

"The Cotes du Rhone? Or the Beaujolais? Which do you think?"

The girl has ruddy cheeks, a trace of baby fat still softening her jaw above the starched white collar. Young enough to be one of his students, and perhaps she was. Or is. "The Beaujolais would be good, I guess."

"With the Filet de Chevreuil? You guess?"

The girl flushes. She tries a smile.

Simon shrugs. Luce can imagine the look on his face, the push and pull of it. "I mean, you'd want something strong and tannic. Something muscular, something that can handle the gaminess."

No smile from the waitress now. She's fiddling with the wine menu, dragging her finger down it like she's going to find the right answer there.

Simon leans forward and gazes up at her. "Something big in the mouth."

The girl's eyes are fixed. She could go either way now: play the game and hope for a good tip, or call the manager. But Simon's gaze can be very blue when he wants something. When he's closing in. He taps the menu. "The Cotes du Rhone is what you'd want. I *guess*."

The girl nods and steps back, nods even as the menu slaps against her breasts. "I can check, okay? I'll check for you, sir, the Beaujolais or the Cote du Rhone."

"Okay." He raises his hands, palms open to show that he means no harm. "Okay, relax. It's no biggie. Whatever you think, I'll go with that." Not smiling now, about to lose interest. She's been too easy.

Luce could leave. There's time; he hasn't seen her.

She could step back, and back, and out the door into the sunlight steaming on wet pavement. She could retrace her steps through the meadow and back to the motel. She could check if they've replenished the mini-bar yet and pop a few pills along with a vodka. She could turn up the air conditioner for its soothing hum, then lie on the bleachy sheets and watch the ceiling to see what happens next. She could tell Simon she forgot the date, or couldn't find the place, or lost track again. He would believe that.

But then Simon turns and grins at her. There was a time she might have suspected a heightened awareness, the same sense of molecular displacement she felt when he entered a room. But then she sees he has seated himself in front of a mirrored wall. Of course. The better to see you first.

He watches her cross the room. She can feel the damp silk clinging and bunching between her thighs, the blister hobbling her left foot, but she smiles and mouths hello. Relaxed. Happy even.

"You look good." He's on his feet now. "Have you lost weight?"

She's considering how to answer that, whether to hug or kiss or seat herself without doing either, when he places a hand on her arm and presses. She sits. His hand slips down her arm and across her wrist, thumb brushing pulse point and circling the mound of her palm. Her blood rises despite herself. But he's looking at her with blue eyes crinkled, chin tucked at just the right angle, and she knows this look, knows what it is supposed to do to her. She slides her hand away.

"Are you hungry?" she asks.

"Don't be like that."

She knows to stay silent, to wait him out.

"We're still married."

"Yes, we are." She tries for her own crinkled eye and tilted chin, then catches sight of herself in the mirror. She looks medicated. "I'm sorry, Simon. This is hard."

"For me too." He leans back. "What do you want? Because you know what I want? I want you well. I want you happy. I want things back to normal. I've been good to you. I've tried to understand, you know that. Jesus, I've been *patient*."

The waiter is back and hovering, eyes darting between the pair of them, alert to any discord and water at the ready.

Simon leans forward and touches Luce's hand. "I want whatever's best for you. You know I'd do anything for you."

The waiter gazes at him, her baby pink lips parted. She's playing her part beautifully.

Simon smiles at the girl, then turns his bluest gaze back to Luce. "Why don't you order? You know what I like."

Luce feels the waiter's eyes on her. The waiter is young enough to envy her, to believe that compliance means consent and either is the same as love. Luce orders, stumbling only a little, on the throatiness of the r and not on what he likes: the foie gras, the filet de chevreuil — and she smiles when she's done. Well and happy and perfectly enunciated.

There's a pause.

"And you, ma'am?"

She doesn't know. Her hands freeze on the menu.

Simon glances at the waiter and grins. The waiter has been welcomed back into the fold. "She'll have the same. We've been married for *ages*."

"How lovely," the waiter says, and scoops up their menus.

The wine comes — the Cotes du Rhone, not the Beaujolais — and Simon waits until the second glass before he asks her how long she needs. To be well and happy. To come back to him. He wants her to know that she has been missed. Her yoga instructor keeps phoning, the faculty dinner is coming up, and they need to make a decision about the timeshare. Old Mrs. McDougall saw him walking Bella alone and left a casserole on the doorstep, something grey and greasy, and not even Bella would eat it. Luce sips her wine and listens to the rise and fall of his voice. It sounds like another woman's life. It sounds appealing and comfortable, like other people's lives so often do. By the third glass of wine, she's laughing at the stories he tells; the bad students and their dumb mistakes, the dumb teachers and their bad accents. *Je t'aime, je l'aime, je m'aime.* Tame, lame, maim. The waiter returns to light the candles and gives them an indulgent smile.

"You're such a gorgeous couple," she says.

And they are. She can see this in the mirror, how the light flickers over her face and his, softening flesh and history and offering return. They could be happy, people like them. *Je t'aime.* She remembers this, when he could say the words and she would forgive him. Simon leans forward and takes her hands in his. Chin tilted, blue eyes luminous. So damn pretty.

"There was a fawn," she says.

But he's working her hands, turning them over in his, thumbs rubbing circles. "We could try again," he says.

"It was too small," she says. Or maybe she just thinks it; it's hard to know with the feel of his skin on hers, with the candle blurring her words.

He's talking. "It's what people do. They move on and try again. We could, we *should*. Once you're well."

His eyes so blue. Once she thought you could figure the soul there, in the eyes.

"There's time," he says. "You're young enough, still."

She wonders what he would do if she blew out the candle. If she tossed her wine in his face, or threw her chair, or screamed loud enough to raise the dead. How he would salvage the show then.

Of course she does none of these things. She calls for the check.

The waiter gives it to Simon and he takes it. He offers to call her a taxi, and nods when she declines. He walks her to the door and down the street, away from the girl and the restaurant window. It's still light out, and the sunset is only a blood-red streak of sky over the horizon.

"The waiter?" she says, "She was just a girl. A baby."

"Don't start," he says.

But he walks with her a little more, and they stop at the place where the path veers from the road. The scent of damp hay rolls off the meadow, and she breathes it in. There's no one around. Simon must feel the seclusion too; his shoulders slump and his face looks parched, thinner. "You have to know. What you're doing to us. It doesn't look good, does it?"

She steps onto the path and turns. The sun is in her eyes. Simon is backlit and shadowy, hard to see.

"I don't know." He sighs, deflates a little more. "What do you want?"

Luce kisses his shadow self. Then she leaves him.

She passes the fawn on the way home. It lies where she's left it, its eye clouded, its belly already swelling. She kneels in the bunch grass and throws up a clump of brutal meat, panting and heaving until nothing more comes.

Luce stays there on her knees and she sees this, a last performance piece: the woman, crouched with her baby until the dark closes in, until the moon rises and shows the silent shape of things. Luce stays, seeing the marbled blue veins and their delicate tracery, how each divergence was a tiny galaxy, expanding, infinite. Holding this like a jewel in her closed mouth, tasting it, turning it over and over.

THE FABULIST

WHERE I GOT YOUR PICTURE is not important. That I thought I needed it? This is what matters.

You stand with a close-mouthed smile and your chest offered, your hands behind your back and a blue tie ringing your neck. You look well fed and important. You look official against a background writ with slogans: Family First, Time to Trust, *Éirinn go Brách*. The article says there's been rumours dogging you but this is to be expected, for you are a charming man. I wonder which acolyte is taking your picture. You look both at her and past her, like she's something you could have but don't really want.

But for that, I never would have recognised you.

I remember you barefoot, sitting cross-legged on a hostel carpet flecked with ash and beer stains, eyes half-mast and a spliff hanging from your mouth. Your cheekbones shone in the dirty light, your eyelashes left spiky shadows. I sat next to you, facing the French boy cultivating *laissez-faire* and a pair of English girls trilling for your attention. Our hands touched when you passed it on, and your knee juddered against mine. You did not look at me. The first thing you ever told me, with your tongue lilting and thrusting on the *t*, was to stop bogarting the joint. I didn't know what you meant but I thought I could taste you when I inhaled. The French boy slumped sideways and the English girls left for the loo and never came back. You rolled another and told me about the horses, about the time you'd stolen a Connemara pony from the Christian Brothers and rode her across the cliffs and how the wind felt, how the wind was more than the fall and the snapped wrist, more than the beating they gave you after. Your eyes half-lidded on me, your tongue thrust and rolling. *Da brudders da wind da horrsses.* It was a given that we would sleep together.

But not for some time. You were a Catholic; you understood how denial fed the sin. I was new world suburban and brought up on low fat and no sugar and the moral imperative of just saying no. The English girls whispered about sex in the showers and who did who in the laundry room with the door blocked with a chair. They said the best place was the roof. The Belgian boys didn't care; they hung their bedding from the top bunk and bumped together behind it, and the Aussies snickered about shagging sheets. The travellers came and went, hooked up and fell apart, and neither of us made a move. We averted our eyes from the grappling and told each other we didn't have the money to leave just yet, that we needed a few more weeks of under-the-table temping, that it was the wrong season for travelling anyway. We went to the museum and the castle and the cathedral, and you read me the words from the pamphlets, your accent rolling and clogging on the plosives. I'd watch you drift between the glass cases, loose-boned and lanky, your hair too long and in your eyes. The young mothers flashed looks over their strollers, the older women stared. It occurred to me you were beautiful. It occurred to me that I was not. But it was me you brought cups of tea night after night while the others spilled beer and threw chips at the telly when the wrong team scored. Your hands were delicate on the porcelain, fine-fingered as you pinched tobacco for your rolling papers. We did not touch.

You sat with me in the fug of old beer and cigarette smoke, and you told me you were going to Greece or Turkey or maybe Ibiza. One of those blue sea and white sand places, where you'd trance out the night and sleep through the day, pick up work in the clubs and move on when you were done. You talked, and your eyes glinted silver when they caught mine. You talked, and I imagined the blood warmth of the Aegean, the rub of desert wind and the spice market stink, the feel of clouds at my feet. Morocco, Rajasthan, Tibet. Each name in your particular pronunciation, claimed by your tongue.

You told me what you had left behind. The horses, and how it was possible, hoofing over sand or flank deep in seawater, to lose the sense of the ground. Your father there one day and gone the next and your mother tight-lipped and clipping coupons. Your big sisters running wild, knee deep in the tidal pools and fists blackberry-stained, wreathing the lambs with foxglove, knuckling your hair and pounding your flesh and stopping your mouth with violet sweeties stolen from the corner shop. Each had fallen pregnant before leaving school and, weighed down and strung out with every child thereafter, had asked you when you'd find a nice girl and do the same.

There was a girl. You told me this with your eyes half-lidded and your hand tracing circles on the carpet. My lips closed over a spliff damp from your mouth. A nice girl. But it was not for you, this doing what was expected. Not without the passion. You'd left.

For what was the point of it, the point of anything at all? Without the passion?

The passion. You watched me like you needed an answer, your eyes a slippery silvery grey. My head floated free, drifted from my body like a rowboat cut from its moorings. My mouth opened, scuttled air. Something clunked under my ribs, dragged through my belly. I passed you the joint.

You took me to the roof later. We stood on tiles sticky with heat, and the air was thick with the scent of coffee and cinnamon, cigarettes and petrol. It could have been any European city on any summer night. I turned to say this and you lifted me right off my feet. Charmed, alarmed, I couldn't speak with your tongue in my mouth.

I remember I did not sleep. Not that night, or the next, or the one after. We built a nest next to the chimney with stolen sheets and cushions, and we hoped it would not rain. The candles were your idea; the light flickered over your closed eyes, the rise and fall of your chest. I played with the wax and memorised the bones of your face. I took in the thumbprint hollow where throat met clavicle, the constellation of freckles marking flesh, the whorl of hair funnelling to curled cock. I thought I would need these things later.

One such night, you brought a bag of peaches from the market. You bit into one and kissed me, and traced the opened fruit over my breasts and belly. Your mouth moved downwards and I told you I loved you.

Of course you left. That too was a given.

You had the wit to do it by degrees. You missed a movie and blamed it on the Belgian boys plying you with moules-frites and beer. You got a job across town and worked the night shift. You moved to a flat full of Australians and told me it was lads only, with dirty cups and never any loo roll. Your tongue stumbled while your hands circled air, and your eyes flickered away. You gave me a phone number that rang and rang when I called.

Of course I got over it. I took what you had left — a grey t-shirt, a pewter lighter, the phone number in your jumbled writing — and zipped it into the hidden pocket of my backpack. I flew home. I told those who asked that I'd had enough of travelling, I'd lost the passion.

I married a nice man. I had two nice kids. They weighed me down and strung me out, they filled me up and shaped my days. I was happy. I forgot you.

But there were moments. Between the tidal flow of meals and dishes, the school run and part-time job, the sore throats and bleeding knees and toothpaste kisses, there were moments. After a party, when I woke to a hand drifting over my hip, with my head floating and throat bubbling *you you it's you* and my husband laughing *of course it is, you ninny, who else would it be?* Another time, when a man at the meat counter in the supermarket asked for lamb chops in your voice. Once, when polishing our dresser with beeswax and a grey rag, as my mouth filled with a taste of acrid smoke. I unrolled the rag and saw the sleeve, a long-ago label fading at the collar, and I had to sit with my head on my knees.

But these were only moments. If I had found your photo then, I would have seen a family man softening into middle age, a minor celebrity from some other place, a face pleasant enough to read the weather. I would have passed you over and picked up the kids from school. I had nothing to purge then.

My husband was an honest man. He preferred fact over fiction, and photographs to paintings. He used his camera to document the time passing through us; the months of my waxing belly, the creep of candles on birthday cakes and the years of our children sprouting up the doorframe. He bought the best editing software available but he had rules. He would not manipulate the truth. I asked him to blur my frown lines once and he scoffed *what do you take me for, a fabulist?* But our Christmas cards were pretty; our kids had gapless teeth and unscraped foreheads, and I looked like I slept well.

I thought of you one late winter day when I was home with a cold, when my husband was at work and the kids were at school. The house was quiet and the day had lost its shape, had come unstrung. I was scrolling through other people's photos on Facebook, comparing their families to mine. I was feeling lucky. I was feeling bored. I wondered if I was happy or simply doing what was expected. When I closed my eyes, it came back; rooftop sticky from heat, the hum of traffic far below, the feel of warm wax. The sound of your voice.

You were easy enough to find. You'd gone home and become a little bit famous; the newspaper called you a prodigal son.

Your photo fills my screen now. You stand with a close-mouthed smile and your chest offered, your hands behind your back. Your silver eyes are hooded and pouched, your curls cropped. There's a blonde woman standing next to you, two tall children flanking you. The caption gives their first names along with your last name. It says the woman was your childhood sweetheart. Family First, Time to Trust, *Éirinn go Brách*.

The walls of our house are bare now. I want you to know that. There are dark shadows where our family photos should be, and the pictures themselves sit facing the wall, shrouded in white sheets. This was the first thing I did when I got home from the hospital.

Your wife will have to go. I crop her and clip away one of your children. The other goes next. Now there's just you, and *Éirinn go Brách*.

You look self-satisfied, despite your losses. The tool bar frames you; a strip of hieroglyphics, a language for the dead. I blow up your face until it pixelates. I smudge shadows under your eyes, darken the hollows under your cheeks and deepen the lines from nose to chin. I swipe the smile from your face and blacken the corners of your mouth. The soft flesh of your jaw I leave hanging. You don't always lose weight with sorrow.

I print out eight copies in full colour, and tape you to every wall of our house. Your face hangs at different angles and heights; you've been called to testify, to bear witness, to buckle under the weight of these silent rooms.

When the dinner hour comes, I sit at the kitchen table with a packet of stale pita crisps and a bottle of wine. Your face hovers, a tragedy mask above the empty chair. I wonder if you ever got to Greece.

We were going to do Europe this summer, did you know that? The whole family. We bought the kids luggage for Christmas; purple metallic for my daughter and a Spiderman wheelie for my son, with the tickets tucked inside. We planned EuroDisney, yes, but also Chartres and the Rijksmuseum and Neuschwanstein castle. My husband looked up the correct pronunciation and fed it to the kids in bite-sized pieces. No one was going to laugh at our accents.

You stare back at me from above the chair.

Da brudders, I say. *Da wind, da horrsses.* You prick.

Silence. I see that your face looks wrong, lopsided. One eye crinkles up more than the other, one side of your mouth smirks while the other turns down. It's not the wine. No one is perfect, the orderly told me, no one is entirely symmetrical. But our eye fills in the blanks because we are made to dodge discord. We tilt towards balance, every time.

I take the wine bottle to the computer. When I am finished cutting and pasting, I have two photos, the halves the same and the wholes different. Your face crinkling up, smirking like a satyr. Your face turned down, cheekbones dull as slabs of meat. The satyr I tape to the living room wall. It's you I want to talk to.

My husband was not a passionate man. He woke when it was his turn to warm the bottle, he arrived on time and left the toilet seat down and took the bins to the curb on recycling day. He remembered the kids' birthdays and picked up ice-cream cakes from the Dairy Queen. On Saturday nights, he touched my collarbone then my nipples right and left. I was not unhappy. You need to know this.

He was an accountant and the son of a wheat farmer, with clean fingernails, but hands as solid as spades. He sat with his hands on his knees, like his father before him, and laughed without making a sound. He took up space. I knew when he entered a room; I could feel the displacement like water banking over the sides of a bathtub. Something settled and locked when he came home, and he always came home. You should know this.

The slab-cheeked you stares up from the desk. You look drugged, inanimate.

The orderly took me to the basement. It got colder as we got closer to the core of the building, as we left the heat of the summer street.

The sheet covered half of my husband's face. He looked wrong, off kilter, unlined and amorphous and less than he was. *I can't be sure*, I told the orderly, and reached out to take the sheet. The orderly held my hand. *The accident*, he said. *It's not possible.*

I lay your halves on the table, meat slab and satyr, side by side. Neither is you. Not really.

I open another bottle of wine and pull up your face on the screen. You're not as I remember. You're not what I want. I soften your shadows. I darken your hair and fill in your temples, erase the hollows under your eyes and blur the lines knotting your forehead. I fill your eyes with a silvery light.

This one I hang in the bedroom. I lie on the bed with the wine bottle nestled between my thighs.

You you it's you. My husband and his solid flesh against mine, my fists kneading his back. My eyes closed and seeing constellations, the glint of silver, the tongue thrust and rolling, telling of horses. Feeling the long lanky bones of you. My husband heavy on my chest after and my traitor hand smoothing the damp hair from his forehead. My gorge rises.

The porcelain of the toilet is cool against my skin. My hair hangs in strings; I can't remember the last time I showered. Like this in front of my husband, three months along and throwing up soda crackers, terrified, sure I would dislodge the kernel of our first child. Weeping and stinking while my husband held my hair and rubbed circles onto my back, and it was not passion. It was not passion and that was the point. You need to know this.

I rinse my face under the tap and wipe it dry. My reflection stares back at me, eyes red and hollow. I want to sleep but I have not finished with you.

Your photos make a tidy pile in the barbecue. The match gives a little snick of anticipation, of birthdays and illicit moments, then the paper catches and flames, high and hot and out in less than a minute. Your smoke clogs my nose and tongue, and I can taste your ashes for some time after.

Toward the end, I woke up and reached for you, and found the sheets cooling around the space where you'd been. A snick of lighter, the catch and flare of your cigarette in the dark. I couldn't tell if you were looking at me, at anything at all. That ember, pulling and receding for a time, then the soft creak of the roof door. I never called you back. I knew better.

Toward the end, I woke up reaching for my husband and felt the displacement. The kids were with my mother; we were supposed to be working it out. I had a long list of evasions and he had a methodical optimism. There was the snick of a dresser drawer, the click of a belt buckle. *Can't sleep*, he murmured. I lay on the bed and listened to the car start. The headlights swept over the bedroom and I never called him back, I never stopped him. I wasn't sure I wanted to. Not then.

I fall asleep on my daughter's bed with the stink of you in my nostrils, and I sleep through the rest of the night and well into the next day. When I wake, I shower and wash my hair. I grind coffee and toast bread and take my plate to the computer.

Your family takes me by surprise. There they are, smiling on the screen; your wife and your boy and girl, clustered around you like last night never happened. Your wife looks resigned. She'll know you, have forgiven you countless times, and stay with you out of love or habit. The boy looks so much like you. Your daughter is not as pretty and her face is wide open, too trusting. She will adore you and you will love her absolutely, for every fabulist needs an accomplice.

They are more than you should have. I want you to know that.

But this, this too: I have more than I deserve. You hold what I lost, and I lost what I would not hold. You were a shit and you were innocent, and I'm as appalling as I am mundane. Balance and counterbalance and the universe doesn't mind which, so long as the whole remains the same.

Maybe you know this, maybe you don't; your close-mouthed smile gives nothing away.

I delete your photo and pick up the phone. I make the arrangements; I choose the lining and the finish and the words for the service. I pay the man who towed the wreckage and another man for a rental car. I unshroud the photos and put them back on the walls. I don't cry but I can feel the place where the tears might be. I call my mother.

I'm okay, I say. Let me talk to them.

My children's voices, small and serious and questioning.

It's okay, I say. I'm here. It's time to come home.

THE HEARTBREAKS

"LET'S GO," MY BROTHER SAID.

He was leaning against the kitchen door, his Levis slung from his hips and his thumbs hooked in his empty belt loops. His white shirt hung open despite the chill in the air. He hadn't bothered to do it up or maybe he couldn't; I'd found a button gleaming on the floor like a pearly tooth when I'd cleaned up after. The tree lights blinked on and off behind us, reflecting on tinsel and dappling his skin with yellow red green. You could barely see the bruises along his cheekbone and jaw, and I'd already taped up the worst of his ribs. Looking at my brother standing there grinning at me, you wouldn't know what had happened. You would not know what we'd done. The Christmas dishes were stacked on the dishrack, the broken glass swept up and the linoleum scrubbed because I'd needed something to do, something to keep my hands busy and my mind from eating itself, something that would put things back together again. After dad started in on Eric.

"Where?" I said.

Eric gave me a slow smile. "We'll take the van, head south across the line. Seattle, Portland, San Francisco. We got family in San Fran."

The tree lights blinked yellow red green. Wait stop go.

My brother shifted, rubbed his ribs. "Fuck it, Jude. Let's just get out of here."

And I went, for I would have followed my brother anywhere in that winter of 1978. Eric grabbed his smokes and was barely stubbing out by the time I'd stuffed his Adidas bag with underwear and socks, a couple of t-shirts — Blondie for me, Led Zep for him, the old Stones shirt both of us wore — and our toothbrushes in the same plastic bag because it didn't matter much if they touched, not back then. My heart was punching like a piston with the need to get out, to go, but I remembered my cherry cola Lipsmacker and a tube of dried-out mascara I had to spit on to use. I was sixteen. I was sixteen, and there might be boys and how this sent my thoughts reeling, away from the broken glass and blood and dead weight of his body, and onto those California surfer boys, who wouldn't know I was too small and too smart, who'd never seen me slinking through the halls of high school with gnawed fingernails and my brain buzzing on smokepit weed. But no matter how I tried for the smirking nonchalance Eric did so well, I still aced algebra and got one hundred percent on history tests, those numbers and names and dates still unrolled under my hand like ticker tape. My brother felt sorry for me and let me roadie for his band. They called me 'Jude' and 'Hey Jude' and 'Don't make it bad', and they passed me beer and smokes. You wouldn't know I wasn't one of them.

I gnawed at my thumbnail while Eric called Dave from our hall phone. I could hear him whispering with his hand cupped against the receiver. "Tell Rob and Mark to get their stuff together, it's happening." My gut twinged; *what was happening?* "Yeah, you can bring Sheri if there's room." Sheri was with Dave now, after the thing with Rob didn't work out and Mark's girlfriend found out about the other thing. Sheri called everyone sweetie and I wasn't sure I liked her.

"Karen," I mouthed. "Get him to call Karen."

Karen was my friend or at least she was in Grade 11 like me, and sometimes we shoplifted nail polish and gum from Woodward's, and once we drank the lemon vodka she'd stolen from her dad's liquor cabinet, and had ended up laughing and screaming and stumbling across the railway tracks and into the woods. Karen fell over when she tried to pee against a log, and passed out flat on her back with her legs beetled out and her feet hooked up in her jeans. She made me walk behind her on the way home to hide the wet patch on her bum. Karen had done it with three boys already or so she'd said, and I hadn't told anyone else because I didn't have anyone to tell, and because I knew what happened after you had sex, what with the pregnancy and heartbreak and insults inked on washroom walls, I didn't want any of that stuff to happen to Karen. So yeah, I guess you could say we were friends.

We kept the tree lights blinking on and off when we left the house. It wouldn't have looked right otherwise.

When we picked up Dave, he had a stupid smirk on his face and Sheri clinging to his arm. Both of them piled into the van in a tangle of arms and legs, with Sheri giggling and wafting Love's Baby Soft perfume over the odour of Dave's smoke-stained jean jacket. Dave pushed up his shades and told us that Rob was spending Christmas in Vancouver with his girlfriend, and Mark was flat out broke again and working graveyard shifts at the mill. Eric let out the slow whistle that meant *yeah, figured as much*, and put the van into reverse. Dave had pulled out his gear and started to roll up before we got to the end of the street.

Karen waved us down from the bus stop and Eric gave her the front seat while I shoved in beside Sheri and Dave. Karen got car sick, or so she said. She sat too close to Eric and flipped through our shoebox of cassette tapes, swinging her long ashy hair and wavering between Blondie and Fleetwood Mac. Eric didn't say anything even though he hated both. He took the tape from Karen and slid it in the player, and when Dreams came on, he sang along in a squeaky falsetto.

Girls liked Eric. They phoned in breathy giggles and showed up at the house looking tear-stained and desperate. They took me aside at school to ask where Eric was playing that weekend and if he had any groupies yet. Sometimes they passed me notes written in strawberry-scented ink, their names in loopy script with heart shapes dotting the 'i's. Karen would read each one and laugh.

"Too easy," she'd say. "Too young, too fat, too dumb. Besides, Eric needs to focus on his music if he's ever going to make it big."

Eric had bleached blond hair that flipped out perfectly and a way of looking at you, all sleepy eyes and parted top lip, before he smiled long and slow. The teachers had called him a dope until he dropped out, and our dad had called him a faggot pretty much ever since. The guy who wrote the music reviews for the local paper called him the poor man's Peter Frampton, a shoo-in for the checkout girls and millworker's wives. The comparison confused Eric. Goes without saying, he'd said, we're all poor round here. But my brother could sling a guitar at the end of a song — Wild Thing, Get it On, Satisfaction — with his hair hanging and his foot kicking the last notes away. Sexy, said the girls.

"Hey Captain," Dave's voice was pinched and thin with pent-up smoke. "Captain Beefheart? Where you taking us, Captain Beefheart?"

"Bee Fart," Sheri giggled. "Oh my God."

Eric ignored them both and addressed me. "I called Larry. You remember Larry?"

I remembered Larry. He was some kind of cousin of ours on our mom's side, one of our relatives who'd drifted in and out of barbecues and weddings, one of the faces at her funeral. Larry had made and broken bands over the years, and he'd hauled heavy equipment for Eric one summer. Larry was a talented beer drinker and he could flip his bottle cap into any receptacle: a trash can, a Styrofoam cup, and once, even Sheri's thrust-up cleavage.

"Larry's stage crewing in San Francisco. At Winterland. Bill Graham's Winterland, I'm not shitting you, Bill fucking Graham."

"Oh my God, like the evangelist? Larry got born again?" Sheri's eyes were wide.

"Not Billy, Bill. Bill Graham's a concert promoter."

Dave sat up, sobering at the name. "No way. You bring our demos?"

Eric grinned at him in the rearview mirror.

"You're gonna be so famous!" Karen poked him in the ribs and only I saw the wince.

"Yeah well, we got to get to the man first. Larry doesn't know if he can swing it, short notice like. But he's going to get us into a concert. He says he can do that. Through the back door maybe, but still. Winterland. In San Francisco." Eric drew the syllables out like when he was teaching me to smoke.

"Who we gonna see?"

"Oh my God, tell me it's Blondie. Or Fleetwood Mac. So bummed I couldn't see them in Vancouver cuz my mom wouldn't let me miss school. Like I would *miss* school." This was Karen, and it was true; I remembered her sulking through most of last September, hiding out in her bedroom and playing the album over and over, turning up the volume until her mother had stomped upstairs and pulled the plug.

"Depends on what day we get there. We missed Springsteen. But Larry said the Grateful Dead's playing on New Year's Eve."

Dave thrust his joint over the front seat. "Better toke up, Captain. You're not stoned enough for the Dead."

"No one's stoned enough for the Dead." Sheri giggled.

Eric inhaled and passed the joint to Karen. "Keep it low," he said to her, "you know how the cops look for any excuse to bust my ass. And no more, Dave, you hear? Van's stinking of weed and we got the border crossing in a couple of hours."

"Jesus. You sound like your dad."

I stiffened. But Eric just grinned and flipped Dave the bird, told Karen to switch the tape to Springsteen. Thunder Road, Tenth Avenue Freeze-out, Born to Run. It didn't matter that it was the dead of winter and getting dark and beginning to snow; when the chorus came on, we all howled along.

You could have called my brother and me cold-blooded. You could have called the others stupid to ask no more questions about where we were going that cold December day, and why. You could have wondered at that. The cops did, later.

The dark chased us through the canyon and gathered in the mountain shadows, and was creeping into the van by the time we passed through Hope. Eric put on the new Springsteen album and the songs were sadder, slower. Karen curled up in the front seat, her feet stretched towards Eric, and Sheri cuddled into Dave. I leaned against the window and closed my eyes, lulled by the slow fall of snow.

Just before the Sumas border crossing, Eric pulled over into a farmyard drive.

"Get rid of your stash," he ordered.

Sheri looked at Dave. Dave stared ahead, glassy-eyed.

"Oh man," he said. "Oh man."

My brother swung around in his seat and glared. "I mean it, Dave. I'm not going through with a couple of minors and a van full of smoke."

I slid open the van door and fanned in the cold manure-scented air.

Dave fumbled in his jean jacket pocket and produced a baggie with a few flakes at the bottom. He shook it at Eric with a currish grin. His teeth were flecked with green.

"You swallowed it?"

Sheri giggled. "When we went through Hope. It's those mountains, they make him nervous."

Eric slapped the steering wheel, and stared ahead, said nothing for a long moment. "Okay. So here's how it's going down. Dave, go back to sleep and Sheri, for the love of Jesus, shut up. Karen, you get in the back seat and Jude, you come up front and look all innocent-like."

"You don't think I look innocent?" Karen tucked her chin and widened her eyes.

Eric gave her a slow grin. "No one's gonna take you for my baby sister. Naw, we're cousins, and we're on the way to Grandma's house for the rest of the holiday."

"Oh man, Gramma's house," said Dave. "Hope she baked cookies."

Sheri's laugh was cut short by Eric's glare.

The border guard waved us through, after a few cursory questions and quick look inside the van, after Eric called him sir and asked him about the weather and the roads and the holiday traffic. His tone was casual yet respectful, the mirror of the voice Dad used when Mom was still alive and we'd haul the trailer across the line to camp at Long Beach. Our parents would spread the picnic blanket over a driftwood tipi and drink cheap jug wine underneath, leaving us to slap around in the waves and poke at the tidal pools, to play pinball on the pier and do pretty much whatever else we wanted. That was when Dad was still okay. Or when Mom was still there to rein him in.

The road seemed longer on the other side. The snow had stopped and the pavement unrolled smoothly under the van's tires, with the white lines glowing like runway lights. A neat line of fences held back the dark of the forest. I pushed up the window vent. The air smelt different here, soft with the promise of the Pacific, sharp with cedar and the excitement of going somewhere.

Eric put Springsteen back into play, and the songs made more sense somehow.

We stopped at a motel late that night, on the outskirts of some nameless town close to the Oregon line. Sheri and Dave took one bed and Karen and I the other. Eric wrapped himself in a couple of blankets and stretched out on the floor. I could sense him there awake after the others were asleep.

"Are you thinking about it?" I whispered.

"Nope."

"We shouldn't have just left him there. Like that. What happens if he wakes up?"

"He sees that we aren't there. He sobers up. Then he gets drunk again. He looks around for something to kick. It's not gonna be me and it's not gonna be you, okay?"

"Still."

"Go to sleep, Jude."

And because it was my brother telling me, I did. Because it was my brother lying on the floor next to me, I didn't ask the other question, the one that had been lodged in my brain all through the trip: what if he *doesn't* wake up?

At some point that night I woke up in a sharp panic, sweating, the teeth of a dream pulling at my limbs. A sense of dread, a terrible black guilt. What if, what if? Eric breathed beside me, slow and steady, and eventually I fell back to sleep.

With morning came the madness of three girls sharing a bathroom, and I forgot to worry when Sheri French-braided my hair and Karen smoothed frosted green eyeshadow on my lids with her pinky. Eric looked up from the map he'd found in the motel reception when I came out, but he said nothing and I felt shrunken somehow, like a little girl playing dress up.

Dave was slumped on the edge of the motel bed, bleary-eyed. He stood up, sat down, stood up again and studied his feet.

"Something's wrong with my shoes," he announced. "They got bigger. Or my feet got smaller."

"You're in the States, sweetie," said Sheri. "The sizes are different here."

"Oh," said Dave, and sat down again.

We were on the road and looking for breakfast before it occurred to me.

"Eric, I don't have any money. I mean, I have ten dollars in my purse. But they don't take Canadian here, do they?"

Karen whispered, "You goof. Didn't you get it changed first?"

Eric looked at her, then at me. "We got enough."

And when he paid for our hamburgers and shakes, I saw the envelope he'd tucked in his jacket pocket, stuffed with the faded green notes. I wondered for the first time if he'd planned this trip, if escape had been in his mind all along.

Karen started in when we crossed the Interstate Bridge into Portland. Not about the bridge, which looked like a lacy undulating caterpillar, but about how she'd always wanted to see the coast, the long-haired surfer boys and big rolling waves, the brown sugar sand and starfish pools, but she never had because her mother was a bitch and never let her go anywhere.

"Interstate's a lot faster." Eric was smiling, but he stared straight ahead.

Karen pouted and snuggled into my brother. "Please?"

Eric laughed, and told her to unfold the map to look for an exit.

Sheri raised an incredulous lip at me. Dave was still sleeping it off and she had no one to talk to.

The coast threw its weather at us; stabbing rain, clouds of fog and a wind so strong the van rocked and bucked. Eric inched along, his hands clenched on the wheel. Karen sucked at a hangnail and even Sheri shut up. We stopped just outside Newport to see the view. Dave grumbled something about cookies when Sheri tried to poke him awake, so we left him the back of the van while we followed a sandy path to the edge of a cliff. The ocean roiled and bucked far beneath the clotted clouds, and the setting sun left threads of dirty blood red. My stomach churned.

"Maybe we should stop for the night." Eric could do that sometimes; catch what I was feeling and say it aloud.

The motel room was cold and clammy, and the foghorn echoed all night long. Karen sighed and jerked next to me, until she announced she couldn't sleep, and that no one could sleep with that damn thing blaring so she was going out for a smoke. The door slammed behind her. Eric swore softly from his place on the floor, then grabbed a blanket and followed. I could hear their muffled voices outside, back and forth in muted argument.

No one was much in a mood for talking the next day. We stopped for lunch at a rundown beach town, its surf shops and hot dog stands boarded up for the season, and spread our gas station sandwiches on a damp picnic table. Karen refused to eat and cast a forlorn look at my brother, her hair whipping around her face, before she announced that she needed some time alone. Sheri said maybe that would be a good idea. The two of them glared at each other before Dave grabbed at Sheri and pulled her onto his lap. I thought of following Karen, started after her even, but the sand dragged at my feet and the surf crashed from the distance. *Sh sh*, it said. All things pass.

I ended up sitting on a driftwood log watching the fog roll in. The jagged rocks receded like shadow puppets behind a gauzy curtain, and I thought of the sailors drawn to the shore, mesmerized.

"Wonder if she found her starfish pool?" Eric eased himself next to me and stretched his legs out in front of him.

I couldn't quite read his tone, so I said nothing.

Eric smiled. "Don't worry about the vibe. Happens when you're on tour; too many people, too little space. Another day, and we're rocking out at Winterland."

"I'm not worried. About that."

"We're here. Oregon beach, checking out the waves, freezing our asses off."

"We have to go back."

Eric was silent. He tapped out a cigarette from his pack and offered me one. I shook my head.

"You know I'm gonna get you out of there, Jude. Soon as we start pulling the bigger gigs, soon as I put aside a bit more money. I never told you this, but I got my eye on a little place next to the lake. Well, a trailer, but a nice one. Two bedrooms. Enough land to have a dog, maybe put in a garden."

And I could see it, my brother and me and a dog, could see the little trailer with yellow curtains and my mom's blue vase on the kitchen table, filled with daisies from the garden. The surf rolled in, *sh sh* all things come to pass and I could see it all so clearly, while the fog funnelled our voices into each other's ears. While it was just us, cut off from the rest.

The fog followed us like a dog all the way down the coast until we crossed into California, where we took a wrong turn at Crescent City and somehow ended up back in Oregon. Karen was moody and silent, but Sheri thought it was hilarious. Eric parked the van next to the state sign, and he and Dave sat on the road barrier, the map spread between them. A cold wind blew through the van, along with a few snowflakes, until a gust snatched the map away and sent it flying into the gulley.

Sheri screamed with laughter.

"Don't worry," I said to Karen. "Eric's a good driver. He can find his way anywhere."

"Except out of Oregon, sweetie," said Sheri.

Dave opened the front door of the van. "Scoot," he told Karen. "Man's job, navigating outta this wilderness." Karen slunk into the back.

Eric climbed in and grinned back at us. He picked up an empty cassette case and spoke into it, in a rich and oily tone. "Good evening, ladies, this is your captain speaking. Weather's fresh with a hint of snow, so sit back and enjoy the ride, while Captain Eric and his trusty co-pilot Dave deliver you through the backwoods of Northern California, straight back to the lights of civilisation." Dave whooped and did a drum roll on the dashboard.

And I wasn't worried, even when we travelled through an endless chain of canyon and forest, mountain and stream, with the only signs of a life a few ramshackle houses appearing at the side of the road and once, a chained dog missing an ear. Dave wanted to put on the Born to Run tape but Eric stopped him, saying we weren't in Springsteen country anymore, so we listened to Fleetwood Mac instead. Something about the hillbilly thump suited the landscape. Karen forgot her mood and waved her arms in the air, undulating prettily like a little hippie girl. Sheri remarked it was crazy how it felt just like Hope, what with the closed-in hills, and Dave said oh man, oh man until Eric told him to shut up. I let it all wash over me, knowing Eric would get us out of this.

When the lights of Crescent City appeared, we all cheered and no one complained about the overpriced and smelly motel room we got there.

Eric called our cousin Larry from the payphone the next morning, stuffing in dimes until the money ran out. When he jumped into the van, he was grinning. "We'll meet him at Winterland when we get in. Couple of local bands playing, Greg something and some guys called the Heartbreaks? Larry says they're good."

And it didn't matter if no-one had heard of either. Sheri and Karen and I sat in the back seat and did each other's hair, applying and reapplying lip gloss, while Dave and Eric discussed how to best meet Bill Graham and which demos to give him first, how to play it cool and not sound like some small town Canadians with cow shit on their heels.

We crossed the Golden Gate Bridge in the dark and it was all lit up like a fairy tale. And it didn't matter if we got lost in the steep hills and narrow turns of San Francisco, if we had to stop and ask for directions, if the city up close was dirty and run down and the fog rolled over the people slumped in doorways. Winterland itself was a huge ugly block, more like a factory than the palace its name suggested. Lines of ragged people were camped outside, rolled in sleeping bags under makeshift cardboard or garbage bag tents. The stink of weed and stale pee was strong in the air.

"Deadheads," sniggered Dave.

Eric did the talking when we reached the front doors. No one seemed to have heard of Larry and they laughed when Eric asked for Bill Graham. The concert had started; we could hear the muffled roar and thumping bass coming from behind the closed auditorium doors. We stood outside shuffling our feet while the Deadheads eyed us suspiciously.

"You looking for Larry? The Canuck?" A big man with a beat up face approached us.

Eric nodded.

"You the other Canucks?"

Eric tried out his slow grin.

"Jesus God. How'd you even find us? They have cities where you're from? Flew over the prairies once on the way to a gig in London and fuck a duck, that's a whole lotta nothing, pardon my French, ladies. You folks come with me, I'll take you to Larry."

He turned and we scrambled after him, past the Deadheads and around the corner and through a rabbit warren of trash and dumpsters. The night air thumped with distorted bass and still the man kept yelling — shitty weather, you guys bring that with you? — until we reached a large set of doors propped open. The sound coming from them was deafening, a mix of thumping bass and jangling guitar, the roar of the crowd.

I thought it was one of the Deadheads at first, coming towards us gaunt and grinning, clothes flapping as he spread his arms in greeting.

"Larry?" Eric was first to realize.

There were hugs and back-slapping all round, and everyone commenting on how much weight Larry had lost; had he taken up jogging? Gone on one of those West Coast diets? We had to scream to be heard.

The big man stomped off — five of them, Larry? Goddamn, this is coming out of your paycheck — and Larry kept twitching towards the open doors, glittery-eyed and nervous. "You missed Greg. Tom's doing his thing."

"Tom?"

"Tom Petty and the Heartbreakers. Been kicking around a while, didja catch them at the Commodore? No? Man, you gotta get out of the sticks! Band's tight and Petty's got something. Yeah, they're gonna be big, big like a nuclear bomb, like a runaway train, like hell I don't know what, and when they hit, you can tell everyone your cousin Larry told you so." He giggled, twitched at the door again, and I realised he was high on something. "I can slip you guys in. I know the guards, they're great guys, real straight up and laid back, you know?"

Larry led us through the doors and into a wall of sound and smoke and heat. The crowd was packed solid, rippling and closing over us like waves. Larry palmed Eric something before he pushed his way back.

"Let's go," yelled Eric and jerked his thumb at the stage. He wrapped his arm around me while Karen clutched at my elbow. I pressed close, feeling the crush of the crowd, and Eric winced. Too late I remembered his bruised ribs. Karen stumbled, and Sheri and Dave were swallowed up behind us. Then we were there, a few rows from the stage. Stabbing keyboards and swampy guitar reached a crescendo before cutting out to the roar of the crowd, before the stage went dark.

A few chords on the piano, and the singer emerged into the light, striding the stage with his white shirt blazing, mike dragging in his wake and intoning like a Bible-belt preacher. He paused and scanned the crowd, called to us and waited for our reply, reached out his arms and welcomed us in. He hung his head and told us we never had nothing and we would never get anything. That all of us would be betrayed. He clutched the mike and stared into crowd, and gave us a slow grin that said love me, love me now.

"He's got them hooked," Eric yelled in my ear, "and he's not even *singing*."

"He's gorgeous. I think?" That was Karen, pulling at my arm.

Another song came through, and another, more swampy guitar and jangly keyboards, and the singer's voice travelled from low and confiding to a reedy plea. It must have been the heat or the smell of weed everywhere, but I felt my body let go, my shoulders unknot and my head float, my stomach unclench for the first time in days. Karen nestled between Eric and me, swaying, and I could smell the motel shampoo she had used earlier that day. Eric swung his head down to say something in her ear, and I felt a flicker of unease, but no more than that. The keyboards and drums switched into something low and hypnotic and the singer stood in bathed in light. The crowd went wild. Growling, pleading, and then head hung low again, almost incoherent; he gave us permission to love him, to leave him, to hurt him. Again I had that lick of unease. I looked up and saw that Eric and Karen were gone.

The crowd closed in on the space. The band went to intermission and somebody passed me a warm beer that tasted musty, and a joint. I took both and inhaled deeply before Sheri's arms wrapped around me. She didn't know where Eric and Karen had gone, washroom maybe, but Dave had found some guys with excellent Acapulco Gold. The band came back on with a new tone, bright and jumpy, and we pumped our arms with the crowd. Then the singer got pulled off the stage.

It happened fast. One moment he'd been telling us how much he loved rock and roll, the next moment he was gone. Sheri whooped. The bass carried on, the crowd rippled and pulled and we were shoved backwards. Someone screamed. I saw Larry at the edge of the stage, arms reaching, and then the singer emerged, stunned and white shirt hanging off him. His eyes met mine for a second and I recoiled.

Something hard and sour curled in my gut at the sight of him under that spotlight, beaten and exposed, and not what he was supposed to be. Then he flung off Larry, and wheeled around the stage, clapping his hands, urging the band to drive harder, faster. Sheri screamed with laughter. "Totally faked, what a con!" And he gave us a slow grin and finished the song with the same swagger and he'd put into the rest of the show.

But I saw the glassy stare, the skinny ribs, the weakness. The bruises coming to bloom under the light. And I had to get out of there before I hit someone.

I watched the rest of the show from the exit door we'd come in from earlier. The security guard glanced at me a few times but let me alone; I probably didn't look like anybody who could hurt someone. The night air chilled my sweaty skin, and time slowed right down. The music split into tiny shards and each flew into my ears on the beat of an insect wing.

My memories of the rest of that night are fragments only, sound bites and snapshots: somehow getting to the parking lot and Dave announcing he was tripping but that loud guy, the one that let us in? Pretty sure that loud guy was Bill fucking Graham and did Eric still have our demos? Eric incredulous, saying no, he'd given them to Larry. And Larry was nowhere to be found and we were supposed to crash at his place, we *had* to crash at his place because we were out of money. Karen clutching for Eric's hand and his fingers wrapping around hers. Sheri holding my hair back while I puked against the van's tire, saying okay sweetie, let it come up. The lights of the Golden Gate bridge, wobbling and blurring, while Eric said that he was okay, Larry had passed him some speed and that should keep him going at least until Portland and Dave better damn well be straight by then. Karen plugging in the Tom Petty and the Heartbreakers tape she'd gotten off some guy who was all over her, or so she said, until Eric came along and saw what was going down. Snatches of music stabbing at me, heart-hurt and swampy, like time looping back in on itself, like we'd never left that place and we were never going to.

Waking some time later to complete dark and silence.

"Hey. You okay?" Eric was shaking my knee. "We put you up front. You were so out of it, Sheri was afraid you were going to choke on your own puke. Real rock star way to go, eh?"

I could hear snoring coming from the back; the seats had been put down and the others were crammed together in a mess of limbs and hair.

My brother talked until we reached the lights of the interstate, then until those lights dimmed under the morning sun. His voice came at me fast and fragmented, and I fell asleep and woke to another idea spooling out of him, or sometimes a different thread altogether. The guitar, what did I think of that guitar? Tight and precise, and those keyboards, wish Rob had been there to hear those keyboards! The drums dragged but maybe it was better that way, laid back and casual, balanced out all that heartbreak stuff. You could swear you'd heard those songs somewhere, you knew where the music was going even if you couldn't quite place the tune. But it wasn't Springsteen, not quite that. Now Tom Petty, he didn't have much of a voice and he wasn't much to look at, no, definitely not Springsteen, but holy shit was he cool. Total confidence. And he talked to the audience, really talked to them. You could see they lapped it up, you could see they all loved him.

He was going to do that, my brother told me. When we got home. He was going to stand on that stage and deliver, throw it out to the audience and reel it back in. That was the key, the thing he'd been missing. The connection. The love.

We made it to Portland with Dave still passed out in the back. Sheri offered to drive but Eric waved her off and popped another pill.

They arrested Eric at the Canadian border, right after the guard looked at his license and barked at all of us to get and spread our arms against the van. Eric was next to me and I saw his legs jittering, the way he shifted from foot to foot. I knew his eyes were bloodshot and he had a few days of stubble lining his face, that he looked like the guy in a cartoon 'Wanted' poster. The cop patted me down and I saw my dad behind my closed eyes. The vomit rose in my throat. I felt the thud of the bottle echoing up my arm, the pretty shatter of glass, I saw the blood oozing like jelly from a donut and how my dad's stringy hair knotted with it. I saw Eric feeling for a heartbeat after we dumped him on the sofa. My voice came out in a shaky hysterical whisper, "It was me, I did it. He started in and he wouldn't stop, and I thought this time, this time he's going to kill Eric."

The cop looked at me. "You talking about abduction of a minor, miss? Cuz if you aren't, I suggest you shut your mouth."

"Oh my God." That was Karen. "My mom is such a *bitch*."

But it was Karen's mom who came and got us, after they took Eric away and impounded the van. Karen screamed at her for most of the trip back and I pieced together most of it, in between the threats and cajoling. That Karen had been seeing my brother. That he had called it off, and I had brought it on again. That Karen's mom didn't want her near Eric, or me, or anyone like us.

"And I do not mean that in an uncharitable way," she said, her knuckles white on the steering wheel. "I know you've had it hard, with your mom and all. But Karen has a future, you know?" She tried to hug me when she dropped me off in front of our house.

My dad barely looked up when I walked in. The TV was blaring and there was a half-empty bottle of scotch by his elbow. Later, he came to my room and stood in the doorway for a minute, swaying a little. I saw the ugly black cross-stitching on his temple and my stomach turned over.

"You're home," he said. "Christ."

When I next looked up, the doorway was empty.

We were all called into the police station to be interviewed about Karen and what Eric had done to her, and I guess we all told pretty much the same story, minus the speed and weed. Eric was out by the end of the week.

He showed up at the house to get his stuff.

My dad stood with his arms crossed, blocking the hall.

"Get out," he said.

My brother gave him that slow grin. "I am."

My dad swore, but he stepped aside.

"Stay cool," Eric said to me, before he left. "I'm coming back for you, soon as I can."

My dad and I passed the rest of that year in silent dinners and separate rooms. I stayed late in the school library and studied, and I hung out with Eric on the weekends, doing my math homework while the band rehearsed. At the end of Grade 12, I was given our school's biggest scholarship. The paper made a big deal of it because I was a girl, the first girl so awarded in our town's history, and one of the reader letters wondered at the wisdom of that given that I was just going to get married and have babies anyway.

Eric stayed with Dave for a while, then Mike and Rob, until they got the van back and went on tour. Little interior towns mainly - Ashcroft and Cache Creek and Quesnel, west to Chilliwack and east to Castlegar - playing dingy pubs and hotel lobbies and once, an Italian wedding reception. They did covers of the Stones and Springsteen and the Steve Miller Band, and a few of their own songs, and my brother flashed his grin and got some press. A Vancouver agent called just before Karen announced she was pregnant. The baby was his, or so she said.

I went away to university, and Eric took Karen to the trailer on the lake. Eric taught guitar at the rec centre, and still gigged from time to time, but money was tight. Karen's parents helped out with the mortgage and bought the baby things, and put a down payment on the new house when the next baby came. I never knew how Eric felt about this. His voice was drawled and casual when I called, and I could hear the slow smile before he answered any kind of personal question. Then Karen would get on the phone and I'd hear the milky minutiae of baby life, interspersed with how good the newest Tom Petty album was, and how gorgeous was he anyway? Could I believe that we'd gone to see him before all this? By then, I was at my first job at a brokerage firm and the trip seemed like somebody else's story, the kind my boss told over drinks to parade his misspent youth.

Sometimes Karen said other things, things about Eric, that made my heart break. How he couldn't sleep. How she was always after him about the weed, seeing how she hated the smell of it in the house and it was no good for the babies. How he spent long hours in the garage, listening to his records and picking along on the guitar. How they'd been the only ones at our dad's funeral and how afterwards, Eric went on a three-day bender. How Dave was the manager of the mill now and Eric had begged him for a job. And what Dave had said to Eric, about moving forward or going under and he'd better decide which.

Eric only spoke of the road trip once, after Larry had come out of rehab, and they'd had some half-baked idea of forming a band together. He'd phoned me to kick around some possible names and ended up drinking on the other end while I went over my accounts and listened. "You remember San Fran?" he'd asked. "Meeting Bill Graham and not even knowing it? Missing the closing of Winterland by one day, biggest goddamn Dead concert ever, six hours long with a free breakfast served the next morning." He'd snorted and I'd heard the snick of another beer can popped. "That's my trouble, Jude. Always wrong place, wrong time, wrong guy on the wrong damn road."

The years passed and I became an investment manager at the firm, where I met the man who was to be my husband, who was to share a house with me in a woodier suburb of

North Vancouver. We were comfortable but not ostentatious; we wore outdoor casual and shopped at Canadian Tire, we joined litter pick-ups in Lynn Canyon on the weekends.

Eric and Karen left the kids behind and visited us one summer in the late nineties. Karen had tickets for a Petty concert and she'd convinced me to go with her, for old time's sake. We left Eric and my husband drinking beer on the patio, talking about the current political scene. Eric's voice was as laconic as always, but my husband's had developed an edge.

The concert hall had none of the smoke and sweat of Winterland so long ago. The joints were still there, but hidden under cupped palms and the odour blown away by the air conditioning. We watched Tom Petty on a suspended screen and heard him through giant stadium speakers, and the man himself was a stick figure on a toy stage. There was none of the swagger and cockiness, and the slow smile seemed disconnected, coming from a face drawn down by life. The songs were familiar from the radio; but they all had a bittersweet edge even when the beat drove them home. Karen grabbed my arm and told me to look around, to feel the love in the crowd. He's just like one of us, she said, and isn't he gorgeous? I thought he looked depressed. When we returned, my husband had gone to bed and Eric was passed out on the sofa. The house stank of weed.

After they'd gone, my husband poured me a glass of wine and told me that he couldn't believe I was from these people, that I was once someone like them. The world's oldest fan girl and her pothead Petty-wannabe boyfriend. I laughed, hating my husband a little.

Sheri was the only one of us that actually met Petty. She'd left Dave shortly after our road trip, and parlayed her giggle into something instantly recognizable to those who watched her morning talk show. She had her face on the downtown billboards and occasionally interviewed the celebrities that passed through Vancouver. Sheri told Tom Petty our road trip story and he flashed her a grin.

That was a long time ago, he said.

"Did you hear the news?" I'm trying to keep my voice casual, but my brother is the one I'd needed to call.

"You okay?"

"I'm fine. But Tom Petty died."

There's a pause on the other end. I can hear the slow suck of Eric inhaling. His weed is medicinal now, something about a bad back and nerve pain.

"Yeah, well," my brother says. "I was always more of a Springsteen man."

And we talk a while longer, about Eric's oldest son who is finally pulling a decent wage at the mill, and his daughter who is going to finish high school at the same time as her own kid, and if he could convince Karen to do the same, they'd have a real hat trick in the family.

It is a pleasant enough conversation, the kind we have these days.

But I dream sometimes. Swampy guitar while the crowd roars a blood beat, the singer pulled out of the churning mass stunned and white-faced before throwing off those who might rescue him. His eyes meet mine and my gut curls in disgust. That he is not what he is supposed to be. I wake with the guilt sitting on my chest like a cat, and I listen for my husband's breath, slow and steady. *Sh sh*, it says. All things come to pass.

THE NIGHT PASSING THROUGH

SUGAR MOON

BUT WE LOVE OUR KIDS, they say when the police come.

The police take in the plastic patio table heaped with beer cans, the overflowing ashtrays and singed sofa, the rusty smear above the kitchen sink. The complete absence of Barbies or Lego, Xbox or Nintendo.

One police officer picks up a phone from the table and turns it over in his hands. This season's model, and barely in the stores yet. *Where did you get this? Looks expensive.*

We would not, the mother protests. *Could not.* Her hands shake as she lights another cigarette. Her sleeve rides up over a pockmarked forearm. The police officers note this without looking at one another. It's not unheard of, this kind of thing. Not around here.

When the parents are cuffed, it's the father who cries.

The news loops through the village, snagging on remembered details: *She never had anything nice to say to those kids. I saw her smack the boy once and the little girl was so skittish, afraid of her own shadow. She's just the stepmother, you know. They're not even hers. Him? Oh, he's got a wandering eye. Already bored, already looking around. Guess she's gone back to her old habits — how do you think she stays so skinny? Did you see her nails? Bitten to the quick. Or scrubbed.* The voices lift in pity and suspicion, and there's more than a little delight spicing the mix. Someone calls the press.

The villagers gather outside the courthouse. It's early in the morning, so early that the moon pokes a hole in the blood-wash sky. This moon has a certain fleshy awareness today, like a lidless eye open and white. None of the villagers look up. None observe the perfect round glut of the moon and none are grateful for what they've got. For what they've been given.

Perhaps they are tired. Those who live here rarely sleep well.

The moon fades away unseen and the villagers look at each other instead. At the branded suede and designer denim, at the gleaming phones held in perfectly manicured hands. At this unexpected visitation of prosperity. *Awesome*, says one of the crasser ones, looking at his neighbour's sneakers, *are those real diamonds?* His eyes lower in respect, before flitting to the next slick of genuine leather and polished gold. No one looks at the shadows between their jostling bodies. No one looks at me.

I'm content to observe. Today I keep my peace, with nothing more than a serene smile. Today I want for nothing. My hand strokes my swollen belly.

One villager falters. I see his gaze dart below the shoulders, to the gaps between husbands and wives, to the elders wrapped in silence. I hear the dry click of his throat as he swallows. *If you're wondering*, he finally says. *I sent Josh away. To his Grandma's house. You can't be too careful.* There's a murmur of agreement and someone else speaks. *My Megan's visiting her big sister down south.* The heads nod at that; down south is far enough away. *Of course, Katelyn's staying with her mom now, no point being here with the school closed.* A low hum at the perfect sense of this, and a red-faced man speaks, spurred by the congenial spirit. *Connor's still away at camp with the Boys Brigade. He's loving it, especially the swimming.*

The villagers quieten. They know as well as I do that it's November and the mountain lake is savage with cold.

The morning rises and the moon disappears under a web of grey sky. The villagers stare at the closed doors of the courthouse and whisper amongst themselves. The man who was once Connor's father goes to the pub. He brings back a round of beer in plastic cups, and the villagers cheer him on. Others plunge their fingers into bags of potato chips, ketchup-flavoured and family-size, donated by the owner of the Handi-Mart after a dip in sales. The store owner smiles and tells everyone that his son's gone to France on a language exchange and the chips are the least he can do, with all that's happened. His teeth gleam with new veneers.

Then a hundred smart phones light up. The villagers draw breath. The authorities are letting the parents talk now. There's a blur of colour on multiple screens, resolving to the mother and father at a long table, flanked by police and surrounded by reporters.

They're our lives, our precious children. Please. The father sits stunned, comb tracks in his hair, and the woman swallows again and again. They've been pushed together for the cameras like a jigsaw with a few pieces missing. The reporter pokes microphones into their pasty faces, hoping for tears, and the three point lighting shines onto skin greased by fast food and despair. *Please. If you know anything.*

The villagers watch and lick red dust from their fingertips. Someone offer prayers. Another brays when the father's elbow knocks the microphone into a farting cacophony. He is shushed, but not before a trickle of laughter works through the gathering.

The screens blink off. They wait.

The doors swing open and the villagers surge, their phones raised. The police chief comes first to part the crowd and demand order. There's a whisper of complaint, and a single piggy snort, but the villagers step back. Then the father appears with his arm over his face. The woman follows. Her glassy eyes wobble and fix, and wobble again. She's lost weight and her cheekbones jut; she's almost luminescent. A sigh wavers through the crowd and a few women reach their hands towards her. *She would not.* That sigh again, like a tide turning. *Could not.*

She passes close enough to me that I can see where they've caked the makeup over her cold sores. Her eyes rise and fasten on mine, and for a moment I think she is going to speak. That she is going to tell.

She does not. The father pulls her away and she's swallowed by the reaching hands, drowned in the flash of bulbs. The crowd strings along behind her.

The judge who might sentence these parents won't find anything to incriminate them. Should she stumble upon a discrepancy in the transcripts, she'll lose her place when the moonlight slices through her window. The light will glance off the back of her hands, silvering her veins, fascinating her mind and eye. The file will sit on the desk in front of her, solid as a fat red toad, and she'll be unable to find it.

She'll report it stolen and go back to staring at her hands. The couple with the missing children will be sent home. The woman will scrub and sweep and pack. Her husband will help. They'll settle into their new home, with its king-size waterbed and patio hot tub, with crayon-free walls and pristine carpets, and they will look at each other like they've just woken from a bad dream.

I have no remorse for what I've done. For what I am. They want it. They ask for it, every time.

The village square is almost empty. The day has eaten the moon, but I can feel its pull in my swollen belly. And something else. I can feel something else here.

My nose twitches. Something's *different*.

That smell: sea salt and sugar cookie and blood-red reek. Children.

They're grouped on the cobblestones, staring into a shop window. The girl stands under the sheltering arm of her father and the mother reaches for the son. Oh yes, they've got good instincts, these parents.

But they're not from the village. The father wears well-fitted boots and the mother is an expensive shade of blonde. They call their children by the folkloric names favoured by the elite, and the children whinny and flute back, their teeth white and prominent. My ears prickle and warm. I've never had such rich blood before.

I follow them to the village bed and breakfast, which has been renovated with expensively shabby antiques since it changed hands. The landlady lets me in, with a mumbled apology and an offer of tea.

"And how is your little one?" I ask. "What was her name now . . . Alice?"

"Alison," says the landlady. Her gaze is fixed on the tea tray. Her pupils have blossomed like bruises.

"Forgive me. I am old. And where is little Alison?"

The tea tray rattles. "In the city. Working in an office. She's met a nice young man, with a good job."

"She's not married him? No visiting grandchildren yet? Oh, I do like the little ones." Age has made me cruel.

The landlady stares at the dull blue teapot. "Away in the city. A nice young man, with a good job," she whispers. There's a sudden sharp smell of urine.

The visitors are expecting a welcome and they are pleased to see me. I am a bit of local colour, a gap-toothed crone bearing a tray of steaming hot tea and sugar-crusted cookies. Their woollens are slung over the radiator and the children are plump and ruddy with health. The girl reaches for a cookie and the mother stops her with a soft hand.

"Oh God, no," she says, "No sweets between meals. Awful for the tooth enamel, simply *hideous*. Not to mention the calories."

It's going to be difficult. These are not local people swayed by the lure of a widescreen or a barmaid's bosom or their very own modular mansion. These ones can buy whatever they want. For a moment, I wish for the old times when it was a simple exchange: an eldest daughter for a winter of fat cattle, a first son for an endless stretch of harvests. A time when the children came and went, a flux and flow as natural as the swell of the moon.

The girl is whining and grizzling now, and the boy tries an experimental snuffle.

"Oh do stop," says the mother, pinching the bridge of her nose. I can see the skin drag under her eyes, the fine lines blossoming at the corners. I can see the shape of her skull under her thinning skin.

"Quiet," says the father. "Do you know how much those teeth cost? I reckon that's why we're here instead of Barbados this year." His incisors gleam crookedly when he smiles at me. He clamps his mouth shut quickly. I sense gaps, something missing inside him.

I begin my words. Imagine this: the rasping and ancient susurration, winding through the ears and nostrils, burrowing down the throat and into the blood, fixing on the hidden and finding the want. There's an awkward moment, when the father thumps me on the back and wants to call an ambulance, but soon he's rocking with his hands on his knees and his eyes black with forgetting. His hand goes to his mouth, his fingers push and pull at his teeth. The mother resists. *Could not*, she mutters, tearing at herself, *should not*.

"I'm sure you could, dear," I tell her. "You know they're bleeding the life out of you. They'll use you up and never thank you; I know what that's like." I pat the back of her hand. She stares at my swollen knuckles and yellowed talons, my age-stained flesh.

I wait.

Soon she's sitting with clumps of blond hair in her lap, glassy-eyed and passive while her heart unknits.

The children have stopped grizzling. They watch me. I offer each a cookie and they take it. Their teeth carve crescents into the sugary flesh.

"The next empty moon. The darkest part of the forest," I say before I leave.

"Yes." The mother's voice is slurred and dull. "It's the right thing to do. It's the *only* thing to do. To keep what we have."

"They were never ours," says the father, still rocking. "Not ours. Not with those teeth."

The girl's mouth opens, spilling sugar crumbs. In the right light, with a certain persuasion, those teeth could be feral. They could be simply *hideous*.

"Daddy?" she asks. "Mommy?"

The mother knots another strand of pale hair around her finger, and pulls.

I walk the village while I wait. The moon is on the wane. It slivers into smaller and smaller shards, and my belly hollows in sympathy.

The news team swarms the narrow streets for a time, framing shot after shot of an empty swing set and closing in on the rain-soaked flowers leaning against a railing. *From this house. The latest, recalling similar disappearances from the same school, from three doors down or across the way or next yard over. An epidemic.* The reporter waits a beat. *A village without children.* The cameraman zooms in on an upper floor window then, letting the black glass speak of empty beds and stale hush.

I almost smile to see how they've got it so wrong. But then my guts clutch with hunger, and I double over, retching. Those passing by give me wide berth. Someone throws a coin at my feet. It glints and wobbles before settling into the shadows.

The moon curves sideways, its smile steadily eroding. The nights are growing darker. I return to the forest.

The news van stops on the way out of the village, at the place where the road meets the darkest stretch of pines. The doors slam.

I stop scratching in the dirt to watch.

The reporter and cameraman get out. They want a shot of the trees, impossibly dark and dense. *Atmospheric*, says the reporter, *symbolic. Dark times and economic failure, profit-mongering and wage-slicing and crippling debt. So the mill's shut down, the mine's over and done. But someone's making money off this. You betcha.*

Northern towns, says the cameraman. *Jesus. Let's get out of here.*

There's so little left of the moon. Still, its light catches a gleam of bone in the dirt before I stuff it into my sack. A bit of gristle left, enough for soup. My belly cramps in anticipation.

The reporter clutches at the cameraman's arm. *Why has no one searched the forest, why has nobody thought of that?*

My stomach rumbles but I do what I must. I undo the drawstring of my sack, and grope through it until my fingers close on a crescent of jawbone. I use its sharp edge to draw shapes in the dirt. A line of circles, waxing and waning. An open eye. A gaping oval that could be a mouth, toothless and screaming.

The moon, the reporter says suddenly. *Look at the moon.*

Both gawp at the sky. The moon slivers the dark like a scythe. The camera slides from the man's hands and cracks when it hits pavement, but neither he nor the reporter break their gaze.

They stay like this until morning. Later, when they talk of the forest or what happened in the village, they will sense that silvery sharp moon in their mouths threatening to slash tongue. The reporter will try to finish her piece regardless and the cameraman will record her doubled over, spitting up blood.

The moon wanes and I forage, my ribs as bare as branches, my wrist bones as sharp as sticks.

The mother of the disappeared children is found sprawled on the bathroom floor of their new house. Her skin is as mottled and cold as the marble beneath her. *Grief*, says her husband when he talks to the police, dry-mouthed and trembling and scratching at his arms. The police look through each of the many rooms, noting the parcels still in plastic, the metallic stink of new electronics. Their boots sink into plush pile and they say nothing. It could have been grief, for these people who have lost so much. It could have been that, an overdose of grief.

I have no regrets. I give them what they want. If they never know what they need, it is not my concern. The moon passes overhead regardless, its pale eye opening and closing in a slow wink.

The moon disappears entirely one night. By now, I'm stuffing lichen into my mouth and brewing soup out of twigs. Still, I hum as I stoke my oven.

They stop on the same dark stretch of road as the news team. There's a slam of Range Rover doors this time.

"It's dark, Daddy," says the girl.

"Don't call me that," he says.

"I'm not going in there, Mommy," says the boy.

"Don't fuss, darling," she says. "It's the right thing to do."

Her hair has grown back, thick and lustrous and naturally blonde. Her skin is luminescent and plump, her eyes shine as they did when she was seventeen. Her husband simply can't keep his hands off her. He smiles more now, and his bite is perfectly symmetrical.

"Look, kids," he says. "I've brought donuts.' He shakes the bag out on the ground and a few rings roll into the night. The children scrabble after them.

The Range Rover drives away, its engine purring.

It's too dark for stars, too dark to find a trail of crumbs by their light. The children hold hands and sniffle.

I can see the glitter of sugar on their white teeth.

PETEY

PETEY WAS BROUGHT HOME in a shoebox stuffed with grass. There were dandelion petals scattered over him like a child's idea of a funeral, and from that alone I should have known. I should have asked. But I did not. I was too glad for the smile on Lily's face, the first I'd seen since the accident.

"I saved him," she said, "He was floppy and he didn't say anything when I picked him up. But he wasn't dead."

"His name is Petey? Did someone tell you that?"

"No, Daddy. It's just what he's *called*." Lily was seven, at that age when whimsy weighed as much as fact, and wishes were a kind of truth.

We found the old cage in the basement and we lined its tray with newspaper. Lily's mother had kept a canary once. It never sang; something about moulting or poor genes or mistakenly being a female. The canary disappeared when Lily was born. The feathers and shit were supposed to be respiratory irritants. Lily's mother had been good at identifying irritants and ridding herself of them. Or leaving them behind . . . she'd packed her bags before Lily had said her first word.

Lily let me pick Petey up from the bottom of the shoebox. He didn't struggle. The weight of him was unsettling, and the way he spread into my palm like a squashed toad was repugnant. The dirt clung to his feathers and I could smell him, damp and faintly rotten. I dumped him into the cage and he crouched at the bottom, staring up at us with one beady eye. I wondered if he was sick.

"He's someone's pet," I said. "They might want him back."

"He's *mine*," said Lily. Her fingers clenched around the bars of the cage, and Petey's beak popped open, exposing a ruby-red tongue.

"Weeep," he said.

I filled the water tube and poured a cup of canary seed from the bag I'd found in the basement. It was probably stale or rancid, or whatever canary seed becomes after seven years. Maybe it would polish Petey off. We could bury him Irish-style, with singing and dancing and toasting to the health of the living. I had a bottle of Jameson in the cupboard just waiting. I put the shoebox near the cage and hoped for the best.

But Petey lived through that night and the next, eating and shitting and chirping his views. I threw a towel over his cage before I went to bed, where I dreamed of shattered glass and splintered bone. My foot would be kicking a phantom brake when I woke.

Sleep was a bastard since the accident.

The counsellor had suggested herbal tea. I preferred to pour myself a whiskey and stand in the door of Lily's room. I'd listen to her breath whisper in and out and inhale the milky stink of her sleep and, after these small comforts, I would sit in the dark of the living room.

Now I had company. The cage bounced on its spring as Petey jabbed at something beneath the towel thrown over him at night. The rustling stopped abruptly when I swatted at the cage. I took another swallow of whisky, liking how it burned my throat. These small things reminded me I was still among the living.

The counsellor had said that Lily should return to school as soon as possible. That a car crash, on top of a maternal desertion, was tearing a hole in Lily's sense of security. That security was the thing I needed to provide, regardless of how I was feeling myself. That it was my responsibility to keep things normal.

So Lily went back to school. I drove and my hands didn't shake too much. When I dropped Lily at the school gate, she made me promise to take care of Petey. I said I would. Of course I did.

The first thing Lily did when she got home was take Petey out of his cage and cradle him, crooning endearments. The bird sat in my daughter's little white hands, blinking slowly and gaping.

"Something's wrong," Lily said. "He's not talking to me. It's like he's still sleeping." She cast a glare in my direction. "Do you talk to him? Do you say his name? You need to say his *name* before he'll answer you."

"Yes. I talked to him this morning. I said Petey, bro, how's it hanging? And he said he misses his family and he wants to go home." I was sick of that raw red mouth, of how it gaped open every time my shadow passed.

"His family dumped him," said Lily. "They don't want him no more, they don't even *believe* in him. That's why he's ours now."

It was irrefutable. Petey was a reject and he belonged with us.

I threw the towel over the cage earlier every night, and started on the whisky while the rustling and twitching came from behind the bars. More often the cage was dead silent. I had the sense of Petey behind the terrycloth, his beady eyes open and glassy.

My dreams worsened. There was the blinding white screech of tires and the silence after, then the feeling of floating above it all. The sense that this was inevitable and what I deserved: the final fuckup, what everything always comes to in the end. There was the moment I looked down and saw Lily's hand lying boneless between us and I could not reach it, and there were the desperate bargains I made then. There was the sound that Lily made when the saw cut metal and she woke, and her hand grasped for mine. *Daddy daddy daddy.*

Daddy. That hand, spread like a starfish. *Don't leave.*

I wasn't going anywhere. Work didn't want me back until my leave of absence was used up and they could fire me properly. I hoped they would have the grace to wait for my next screwup; if not, there were plenty in the past to choose from. I was home, and so was Petey. We didn't talk much. Petey seemed in a permanent stupor. Maybe the birdseed had some kind of hallucinogenic mould on it. The only time he came to life was when I stuck his cage on the kitchen counter in order to clean it. Then he would squawk and batter himself against the bars as if he couldn't believe he was still alive and was testing his luck.

It was bound to happen, with him flapping against the cage door like that.

I stared at the bundle of sunny feathers on the kitchen floor, and prodded it with my toe. Petey blinked and gasped. His neck was wrenched at an odd angle and his wings were spread limp as a crucifixion. It would be a pity to leave him that way. It would be cruel.

My slipper has a hard sole, for comfort and support. I did not enjoy what I did next, not quite. But my slipper came out clean enough when I wiped it with the dishcloth and we still had the shoebox. I buried Petey in the garden.

"Sweetie," I said when I picked Lily up from school. "Sweetie, something's happened."

"No," she said, with her bottom lip out and her eyes threatening tears. "No it *hasn't*, Daddy."

A shoebox showed up at the foot of my bed the next morning. There were smudges of dirt on the cardboard, a damp patch on the lid. It had rained during the night.

My head floated and I seemed to be looking down from a great height. I wondered how much I'd had to drink the day before. I wondered if I was still slightly drunk.

The shoebox rustled. "Weep," came Petey's voice.

Petey was back in his cage by the time I made Lily her breakfast. Scrambled eggs, with a squirt of barbecue sauce, the way she liked. My hands shook but I didn't puke. We did not discuss Petey.

Lily turned to me when I dropped her off at school. "Remember to talk to him. He likes it when you're nice to him."

I fed him and watered him, but I needed a fistful of Glenlivet before I could start a conversation with Petey.

"Music," I told Lily, "that's what we talk about. Petey likes dubstep.'" I pronounced my sibilants with care.

And I dreamed. Of choking on blood and the bright white light and Lily's hand clutching for mine. How I reached and was grateful.

The next time I cleaned Petey's cage, I left the wire door open. There was a fluttery feeling in my stomach like dread, or perhaps anticipation. Petey scrabbled across the countertop and cocked his head, looking up at me. There was no fear, nothing at all in his black eye. Then he fell to the floor. He huddled, stunned, and began to drag himself along to my slippered foot almost like he wanted something from me. I watched my foot recoil, then snap forwards. There was a solid thonk. Petey slid down the kitchen wall, leaving a smudge of feathers in his wake. I stared at the slumped pile of yellow. It might have happened by accident. I would get Lily a hamster as an apology.

Then the neck unkinked and the feathers fluffed. Petey blinked at me.

"Weeep," he said.

I talked to Lily that night. I was firm. I told her that Petey would have to go; he had a family elsewhere and he belonged with them. His feathers made me sneeze. His crap could give her pneumonia. He wasn't happy with us; he never sang and he barely moved. Lily listened to each of these reasons with admirable stoicism. Or that's what I thought.

She helped me pin posters to the streetlamps outside our house. She even seemed cheerful about it, and I wondered if Petey had outlived his appeal for her. Maybe she was ready for a hamster or a rabbit, something fluffy and bland, and easy to pick up from the pet store.

Of course no one called. I went out one night to pick up a six pack from the 7-11, and saw that the posters were gone. A few tattered strips clung to the tape, resistant to the wind perhaps, or just out of reach for a small hand.

I wanted to question Lily, but when I looked at her over a plate of Kraft Dinner, I saw the hollows marking her face, the paleness of her skin. I saw how her eyes followed my movements around the kitchen and how she wouldn't eat until I sat down and cracked open a can of beer. Petey stared at us from his perch, still as ever, looking for all the world like a taxidermist's specimen. I decided to try a different tack.

"Sweetie, I know you love Petey. I know you want the best for him and you'd never want him to hurt or suffer, right?"

"He isn't hurt. I saved him."

"I know that. But he doesn't really act like a normal bird, does he? He doesn't sing or chirp or peck at his cuttlebone. He doesn't bounce around or flutter at his bars. He doesn't even seem to like us."

Lily's lip trembled. I felt like a shit.

"Sweetie, listen. I think Petey is sick. He might not live very long. I want you to know that, and not be very sad if he dies."

Lily pushed her chair back from the table. Later that evening I found the door of Petey's cage open and Lily kneeling on the floor. She had the bird cradled to her breast, her lips nestled in his feathers. I remembered the rotten meat smell of him and felt my stomach churn.

"Petey, Petey Pete," she was crooning, "you can't leave. I won't let you."

The next time I cleaned Petey's cage, I wore my workboots. He scuttled across the counter and I swept him to the floor, quick and casual, before I could think about it. My foot pumped up and down like easing a brake, and I didn't stop until the bones snapped and the feathers floated. Silence, except for my rasping breath. I would need to look, to make sure. I would need another shot of whiskey. I downed my glass and lifted my foot. A few feathers stuck to my sole and the rest fanned out from what was left, like a lunatic garnish on a plate of mashed beets. Then one feather lazily twirled towards another, and another, until there was a mass of them knitting together like a film run backwards. The ribcage formed under the pulsating yellow, the chest plumped out and quavered as the pea-sized heart began to beat. Petey's red mouth gasped and I scooped him into his cage, winding the towel tight around the bars so I didn't have to see his eyes.

At night I dreamed of the crash and the light. I felt my ribs splintering and my lungs filling and my heart stuttering, the profound snap as I let go and floated above it all. I felt the pull of Lily's hand and turned to look at her. *Daddy daddy daddy*, she said, *you can't. I won't let you.* Her eyes were a beady black.

When I poured my first shot of whiskey later, I lifted the towel from the cage. Petey crouched on his perch and his gaze mocked me.

That same black eye glared at me from the bottom of a Ziploc bag the next morning. I dumped the bag on the kitchen floor and took the mallet to him, the one I used to crack walnuts and flatten chicken breasts, and I didn't stop until the plastic glistened with something like the seeds of a pomegranate. I crouched, nauseous, and waited.

Not a flutter, nor a twitch.

I dumped the bits under the apple tree.

"Please," I said to Lily, "you have to let him go."

"I can't," she said. "He's *mine*."

I thought of the counsellor, peering over her gold frames and lecturing me about my responsibilities. Security, normalcy. Such small things, really.

I dreamed of dirt that night. Of rich brown dirt swirling and squirming into ridiculous forms, like a child's drawing of the Creation; a spotted sponge in unlikely neon, a beetle with a flowered shell, a toad smiling toothlessly before it sprouted canary yellow feathers.

There was a shoebox at the bottom of my bed that morning. Poppy petals this time; it was June and the neighbour's garden was in full bloom.

I spread clean newspaper at the bottom of the cage, and filled the drinking tube with fresh water.

"Weeep," said Petey, and I did. I did.

I talk to Petey when Lily is at school. I don't think he cares much for my opinions, but he doesn't hold a grudge.

I sit in the living room at night, nursing a whiskey or two. Never three. I don't want to fall asleep. I'm afraid I might dream of the crash and Lily's hand reaching, of my ruptured cells plumping while my bones knit together.

The whisky doesn't wash the taste of dirt from my mouth. Petey's cage bounces and I raise my glass, glad for his company. My old pal Petey, the one I knew first. The rest of them rustle and creep around in the dark: a nestling robin bald and bulging-eyed, a clutch of moths and beetles, a cat that crouches flat-eared. There's even a raccoon. He sits on his haunches and stares at his paws, like an old man studying his hands for answers. I hardly notice the smell now. I catch it coming off my own skin sometimes.

It's companionable enough, this sitting in the dark. This waiting for Lily to wake.

LOGGING THE BLACK SPRUCE

MY DAD LOGGED THE BLACK SPRUCE. He wore a cruiser vest, drank Black Ice warm and told ghost stories to hard-knuckled men. So maybe he scared the hell out of us when we were kids, but he was a favourite at the camp. That was something.

He'd come back on a Friday night smelling of pitch and engine oil and rank hair grease. We'd watch him dunk his head under the mudroom tap and scrub his face and hair and forearms with bar soap. Mom put out the flowered towel especially for him, but he wiped himself with his jackshirt and left it balled up on top of the washing machine. He'd stomp past us in his boot socks, whistling loud, thumping his high tight belly with the flat of his fist while he ranged around the kitchen.

"Hey Donna? Hungry as a bear, whatcha got going?"

He liked meat. Not deer or moose, not even elk, none of that backwoods poverty crap. Beef: bright red slabs of supermarket steak mom would buy with the last of the weekly cash and marinate in a bowl of jug wine and vinegar. She'd offer him the thickest cut and he'd mop up the blood with spongey white bread and throw the crusts over his peas, and clunk his spoon off our heads when we did the same.

I'm making him sound like an asshole. He wasn't. He had big hands, scored with splinters pushing their way out in pus, but all his fingers were still there. That was something, considering his work. I remember hockey night on Saturdays after supper, and if the Flames were nailing it, a big hand would drift down and rest on one of our heads. We'd square up best we could under the weight.

The stories came at bedtime. If we were quick to scrub up, if we passed by mom first and breathed toothpaste fumes into her face.

"Yah, okay, minty fresh," she'd say and swat us away. "Ron? You tell them something nice this time; I'm not washing the sheets all over again."

Dad would fix us with his bear-eyed glare, but he'd clamber into bed between me and my brother and clamp our heads with his meaty paws. We'd settle into his chest and listen to the growl and echo of his voice. It was something, that voice.

"I tell you the one about the bucker split his head open in a kickback accident?"

He had, but we stayed quiet.

"Found him sitting on a stump trying to hold his face together. Chrissakes, what a mess. Blood all over hell's half acre and he's mumbling, 'Hey Vera, don't you worry none, Vera, it's all gonna come out in the wash.' We couldn't do nothing for him and the poor guy bled out on the way to town. So. We get this replacement bucker. Guy's half Blackfoot, don't say much but got that look about him, like he knows a helluva lot more than he's telling. So he quits after a week and we ask him, hey chief, what's the story? You know what he says?"

We did, but we kept our mouths shut.

"He says, he says he can't stand that guy with his head in his hands and his ass parked on a stump. Doesn't do a lick of work and never shuts up about Vera."

A long silence. Then Dad would burst out laughing and we would echo him, our faces mushed to his chest. Head in his hands, ass on a stump. Vera. But we knew not to laugh about kickback; that wasn't funny.

Dad would shift position and we would wait, perfectly still, listening to his breath rumbling in and out.

"And the faller, out there in the middle of a cut block? You hear that one?"

I'd glance across at my brother, who'd have his eyes half-closed and a thumb in his mouth.

"So it's first thing in the morning and no one around and the faller's looking at the stand, planning his approach or maybe just scratching his balls, yah, who knows with fallers. Next thing he knows he's waking up in hospital, with a helluva headache and missing every day of that week ending with 'y'. They show him his hard hat, it's been split in two. He can't remember nothing. So I check out the cut block. And what do I find? Nothing. Nothing there, nothing that coulda done that, no deadfall, no unstable slope. Nothing."

We knew our lines.

"Sasquatch!"

"Meteorite!"

"Meteorite? Chrissakes."

My dad would grunt at my brother, then cuff him gently on the head and pull us in closer for the next story.

"This one's mine. This one happened to me."

We'd quiet down. It had happened to him. This was something; this was the truth.

"So I'm end of a shift cutting swamp. It's end of the day and end of the week and I just want to come home to your mom. Swamp can do a number on you, yah? Nothing there but black spruce, and that black spruce is all the same. Bunched and poking up like fingers. Nothing but shadow underneath. You can lose time in the swamp. You can lose your way. And it's getting dark. But I want to get the job done so I keep going. Finally I cut my saw, and when the echo fades there's this silence. No birds, no bush noise, not even the wind. But I get a feeling of something there. Moose, I'm thinking, grizzly maybe. Something standing dead still, checking me out. The rifle's in the truck and the truck's across the swamp, and there's a couple hundred feet between me and it. I haul ass. I think I got time, if what's coming is far enough away. But the truck isn't where I left it. I do a full 360, then again, eyes going tick tick tick, passing along the treeline like hands on a clock. No truck. Even worse, I can't see the road I came in on. Damn swamp spruce looks all the same. It's getting dark; it feels like hours since I finished up. I start walking. I walked outta worse. I know you gotta keep moving. I stop after ten minutes, fifteen maybe, and I'm no farther out of the swamp. By now I'm spooked. I feel like turning on my chainsaw just for the company, you know? It's so damn *quiet*. So that's when I see him. He's standing on a log with his head hanging. Light's gone now, but I can tell he's old by the way he holds himself . . . shoulders sunk in, hands picking at nothing. Too old to be out there. I call out "Hi howya!" and he don't say nothing back. And I'm thinking maybe he's deaf . . . maybe he's an old prospector or a bush elder, and he's wandered off and got himself lost. Could be somebody's looking for him right now. So I'm about to holler again when I notice something else. Something about the way he's standing. He don't have any boots on. His feet are bone white and bare, and he's got his toes curled over the log like he swooped in and landed there. Like he's got reason to be in the middle of that damn swamp with the dark closing in. And I'm thinking what if he's not lost? What if he's just *waiting*? Then he raises his head and I know he's gonna look at me and I don't even stop to think, I pull the cord on the chainsaw. Next thing I know, I'm standing by the truck. Chainsaw still going."

"Did you kill him?" My brother asked once.

"Chrissakes. You think I could?" My dad stared at my brother but it was me he was talking to.

We grew older and Dad stopped tucking us in for the night. We forgot the story of the old man, and the Sasquatch and the kickback. Dad's back slipped a few notches, and he left the black spruce for a lumberyard where he sold lengths of wood laced together with strapping tape and stories. We got jobs and we got married, and by the time my brother's oldest and my youngest were in university, Dad was repeating the plots of sitcoms like they'd happened to him. The neighbour found him in the driveway one morning, hip cracked on the concrete. He'd been up the ladder after a wasp's nest. The damn things were getting into the house and buzzing around his head, keeping him up half the night and 'scaring the hell outta Donna.' It was November and mom had been dead since the spring.

The nursing home is nice one. They have a real tree for Christmas and daffodils in purple vases for Easter. They keep pods of air freshener plugged into the sockets so you can't smell anything over the scent of pine. My dad parks his wheelchair in the lounge and sits in it with his big hands worrying his cuffs and his belly like a flat tire. He keeps kicking off his foam slippers and his long toes curl over his footrest. The nurses say he isn't any trouble.

Sometimes my brother phones to ask if I want to visit Dad. I tell my wife I need tiles for the roof or gas for the lawnmower or a walk to clear my head. I don't know what my brother tells his family. We find Dad in the lounge and I pull up a chair. My brother parks himself on the sofa arm and jiggles his knee. We wait for Dad to begin.

Sometimes he talks of his logging days, pranks and grudges, the big equipment and the bad accidents. Kickback and cut blocks. The old stories. Most days he says nothing. A few weeks back he hadn't greeted us, hadn't seemed to know us. He'd stared out the window, his eyes watery and his fingers plucking. Bewildered.

"Seen the old man last night. Just standing there. Why don't he talk to me, say something?"

We'd told him we were here, we would talk to him.

His hand had slapped his paper cup of apple juice and the liquid had hit the floor like a puddle of pee. We'd called the nurse and left, not looking at each other.

"You remember that story?" my brother had asked in the elevator.

"Yeah."

"What do you think he saw?"

I'd stayed quiet. I couldn't give him the answer he wanted.

Today Dad is calm. The nurses say he's had a good night, he's on new meds. His hands are still now and his fingers curl over the padded armrests. His gaze passes over me and my brother, over the muted television to the rubber tree to the darkened window.

"Old man. Just standing there, don't say a damn thing."

His eyes tick across the wall to the door, making a full sweep of the room until they come back to the window.

"Says nothing, but he sees me. He sees me. That's something, yah?"

THE HITCHHIKER

WHEN I CLOSE MY EYES, I see the moon. I see the moon with its bruised skin glowing and its mouth fallen in, with its eyes pitted and sightless as a potato. I see its high distant sheen and the darkness lying beneath. On nights like these, I go driving.

The moon is full, or it is not there at all, or it is impossible to tell behind a scud of night clouds. Sometimes the air sticks to my skin, other times the cold scrapes at my nostrils and throat. The pavement is slicked with rain or dull with heat, scattered with brittle leaves or sticky with small deaths. She would have mourned them, these clumps of dumb scales and unlucky fur. She was the kind of girl who'd bury a cricket found behind the radiator in spring, who'd swear she'd heard it chirp its death song in November.

I drive out of our suburbs with the streetlights ticking by as steady as a metronome, past the buffer zone of parks and factory outlets, and into the industrial estates. Here there are chain link fences and shadows, the occasional camera mounted high up on a steel pike. One of those cameras took her last portrait. The moon was extraordinarily bright that night; it gleamed off her bare legs under denim shorts and caught on the sparkly bag over her shoulder. She wasn't dressed for the April weather and they didn't think that she'd planned to be gone long. The last message on her phone was to her best friend. Don't find love, it said. Let love find you. Her screensaver was a sunset, overlaid with words looped in some ornate script. *Everything affects everything.* They'd found the phone in a vacant lot next to the sewage treatment plant.

The shadows mesh together under the moon, the parking lights, the lit up factories. Here a criss-cross of chain link, there a smudge of an elm still standing. I look for movement and see the glimmer of a crushed chip wrapper or a tattered plastic bag waving from the dead brush. I drive and I look for the rolling walk, the flash of pale skin.

Sometimes when the moon is bright and the light is right, I see her.

I coast to a stop and pop the passenger door. I wait.

There's the sigh of air, the soft weight of her settling next to me. Sometimes she laughs, more often there's a crinkle of foil and a snick of her lighter as she sparks up a cigarette. She's not supposed to smoke but we are past pretending now.

I know better than to look at her.

I turn the ignition and roll back onto the road. I focus on the white centre line until the shadows blur, until the periphery is a dark tunnel, and I am the one who is still while the world moves through me.

I can smell her shower gel, the one she'd used that evening, under the cigarette smoke. Vanilla Bliss. Fruity shampoo and a hint of cherry lip gloss; the scent of her bedroom when I'd dump her laundry on the bed. "Fold your own damn clothes," I'd say. "I'm not your mother."

"I know *that*," she'd say, and smile, and ask me to make lasagne for dinner, or drive her to the pool, or lend her a twenty for the school dance. Not fooled by the gruff daddy act.

I drive, and I wait for her to talk.

I wait, because I've learned after that first time. The moonlight, the gleam of sequins and the flash of her long white legs, and how I'd lurched to a stop, how I'd called after her until my voice cawed like a crow, until the dark closed in on nothing. The second time was different. I'd sworn to keep going, to get through it, but my heart had been pulled like water down a drain and I'd had to stop, throw open the door and let the night air fill my lungs. When I'd shifted back onto the road her hand closed over my wrist and I nearly swerved into the ditch. How she'd laughed.

And I'd talked, then. My words unspooled like barbed wire, tearing chunks of throat and gibbets of tongue in between the tears and snot.

What were you thinking, what were you doing out there alone?

Who, I'd asked. Who was it? Some rat ass boy? A man? Was it a man?

Was it your mother? Was it something she did, something she said?

Was it me?

Why did you leave me?

Why did you?

Why?

And when I'd finished talking, the seat was empty. I pulled over to make sure, to check the back and put my hand on the leather. Cold. Nothing but the old blood stink of my grief in the car.

So now I drive and stay silent.

There's the exhale of her cigarette. A waft of vanilla. I sense her smiling in the dark.

I write down what she says when I get home. I have quite the collection.

My thumbs, daddy. The world is decided by my thumbs on a 6 by 3 screen, oh those instant likes and casual cuts, you don't know. What it's like.

I like my skin to look airbrushed and my hair glossed. I want to be as smooth as those girls in the magazines. I suck in my stomach until it's concave and I shadow my eyes to show their want.

What I want? I want what everyone wants. I want to be loved to be known to be understood.

Just kidding. I want ice cream, I want to eat ice cream until my brain grows stalactites and my gut freezes fast, but I still want to be skinny. I want to dance crazy-like in the living room and try on all your ties and scream with the weather, I want to do all this without my Adderall being upped. I want to plug in my music and drown out your voices, I want to do this without anyone bitching about depression.

My music, daddy. My music comes from girls with flowers in their hair and tigers at their feet, who sing of a pretty death.

My art, daddy? My art is the dirty words we scrawl on crumbling brick of the bridge.

My art is the razor notches on my thighs, oh God, daddy how I love those little mouths chafing against my jeans.

My art is denial.

But daddy, don't worry. I'm fine. I'm good.

I was never a problem, was I?

Tonight my daughter is quiet. She reaches forward to tap her cigarette into the empty Starbucks mug I've left in the cup holder. I think I see a flash of white wrist but I don't look too hard. I drive past the furniture warehouse and I concentrate on the white line, on stilling my breathing. We haven't got much time left.

Do you ever go into my room? she says.

Sometimes.

Did you find the weed?

It doesn't matter. I'm trying to keep my voice steady.

Bet you smoked it. She laughs. *You dork.*

Something scurries across the road, pauses, wings back the other way.

Sometimes when I was stoned? I used to think I heard the waves coming in, going out. Do you remember when you and mom took us to Tofino? When we were all still together? That was the best. The waves, they were so big they sucked the sand out from under our feet and we couldn't tell what was moving, us or the water. You kept screaming at us to come in. Jason got that rash, sand fleas or something, but mom thought it was measles and totally freaked, and you went to get ice cream. Like that was going to help.

She laughs, exhales. *But it was better. When we were all together.*

I know.

Your girlfriend's stupid. She smells like Juicy Fruit and thinks 'inneresting' is a word.

I know.

But whatever. If she makes you happy.

Was it that, I want to ask. Did you go because of her?

The lights of the sewage treatment plant are coming up, their grid work of lights faint stars in the haze.

It wasn't her. That night. She wasn't even there, remember? My daughter can sometimes read me, hang the answers on the hooks I leave in the night. If I stay silent. *You remember what you said to me? That night?*

No.

I can feel her fading, floating free with every turn of the tires.

Tell me.

Please.

But she's gone. I pull over so I can lean my head on the steering wheel, so I can remember the sound of her voice, so I can replay her words until they've worn a groove through my brain.

I'm in no hurry to be home, to turn out the lights and lock in the night, to dream. To dream of her sauntering away from me, plugged in and heedless of the road falling away ahead, deaf to the crashing waves from some place impossibly far below. I open my mouth to scream a warning and the sand tumbles out. Sometimes I dream of silence. A scatter of bones in a ditch, bindweed knotting through the slats of a ribcage.

I will do this drive again. Some night when the moon is full or slivered or not there at all, a black hole hung in its place. I will stop under the high hazy glare of the industrial lights, and lean across the seat to pop open the door. I will wait.

She'll get in with a rush of shampoo and vanilla. Maybe she'll be smoking, maybe she won't.

Do you remember? she'll ask. *What you said, that night?*

No, I'll say. Tell me.

She'll laugh. *You were in a crappy mood. On your third beer.*

Tell me.

Love. You said love is nothing. You said love fades along with everything else. That the idea of love sours and the flesh falls off it. That love is an invention of the young, something to sugarcoat the shit to come.

I'll concentrate on my driving. On the white line leading into the darkness.

Oh daddy, she'll laugh. *Love is everything.*

And I'll drive, I'll drive until her laughter dissolves in the dark and the white line blurs and floats upward, until the moon appears or does not. Until I am not sure whether it is me moving or the night passing through.

WEIGHTING DOWN THE DARK

SACRIFICE

THE OTHERS HAD FELT IT coming. Afterwards, they would each describe a sudden pull towards their children, an urge to call someone, a kind of thrum along the spider silk that connected them to their families. Each knew it to be a warning, but would not mention it out loud, *because*. Because such warnings came a dime a dozen to mothers. Because they saw these things on the news daily. Because to say it out loud could draw it here, could make it happen to them and their children. Afterwards, each would be able to pinpoint the thing they did differently that day, the subtle adjustment they made so that their families remained intact. But Rachel had felt nothing.

Rachel remembers this: it's a day early in spring, the kind of day that delights in contradicting itself. Here and there a tuft of virgin grass sprouts while drifts of old snow cling in the shade, and the stench of spongy lawns and thawing dog turds mingles with an almost Mediterranean scent of box hedges. Not that Rachel would know what the Mediterranean smells like, but she imagines it to be a cross between dried rosemary and the Song of Santorini bath oil she uses on a Tuesday night because this is their night, the night he is most likely to call. Or it was. Before. But now the robins have returned home; they're bunched together in the greening branches, rusty-voiced and querulous before pairing for the nesting season. The weather is mild enough to walk to work, and she is doing so with a case of cupcakes clenched in one hand, careful not to jostle them because the icing is still soft and likely to smear. The children carol from the playground, unzipped and bareheaded, for there's some heat to the sun. A clattering skateboard startles her and the cupcakes slam against her thigh. A boy in baggy shorts calls something over his shoulder . . . *cruise by? so fly?* . . . and rattle-thumps from the sidewalk to the street, and she thinks he could have been hers if she had gone through with it, if things had turned out differently. *Oh but you're so gentle, so calm!* the women at the office say, *why didn't you have babies?* That low confiding tone, that stabbing sympathy. Rachel always laughs and blames a surfeit of steadfast men, or casts her eyes down and hints at biological disappointment. But what could she have done given the circumstances? She holds her clutch of cupcakes tight and thinks it's just as well she's nestled sugar eggs in the pastel icing. Today is the first day of spring break and there may be children visiting the office.

She remembers how the sun looks when she arrives at the office, how it glints off the winter litter caught in the bare flower pots, how the light hits the glass and exposes the smudge marks. There's a child's handprint, a perfect palm with each joint articulated, just under the door handle. She remembers this, and the instant check of heart . . . *am I charmed annoyed struck with grief* . . . and the decision to feel none of these things.

Simone smiles up from reception and hands Rachel her new claims. Simone's little daughter is rummaging through the toy box in reception, thumping toy cars together like she's cracking heads.

"Visit mommy at work day," says Simone. "Unofficial."

This is the code around the office for a failure in arranged childcare. No one minds; the babies are passed from arm to arm and everyone exclaims at the size of the boys and eyelashes on the girls.

"Rache!" Peter descends upon her, his eyes wide and his white teeth bared. He flings his arms out for a hug and finds the cupcake case instead. "What have you brought today? Give us a look!"

"Shush, let her get her coat off." This is Andrea, Peter's sister, dragging her long gauzy skirts in his wake. She picks at her nose ring then hoists her waistband up over her belly. "Did you have a nice weekend, Rachel? Go anywhere exciting? Oh I can't imagine how it would be, to be able to just take *off*! And you had time to bake cupcakes too!" She grabs the case from her brother and dumps it on the counter. "Piss off, Peter. You'll just complain about getting fat."

"You should talk," Peter huffs and sucks in his stomach. His jeans are too tight, too short, but Rachel thinks this is intentional, some kind of thrift shop chic favoured by the young. His sister appears to have wandered away from some music festival befuddled and blinking, amazed to find herself pregnant yet again. She has an oddly calming effect on their most difficult clients. But the piercings and the swearing, the drifting around the office while the files pile up! Rachel can't help thinking that if she acted like either

Andrea or Peter she would be canned. But she tries not to think like that, she really does. It makes her feel old.

"Haven't you got something to do?" Simone glares at Peter, who is pawing the lid off the cupcake case.

"Oh it's fine," says Rachel. "Really, they're nothing special. I thought, well, Monday and all, right?" She flashes a smile at Simone; it's important in this office to look like you haven't tried too hard. To look like sugar eggs were just something you happened to have lying around.

Simone ignores her, her gaze clamped on Peter.

Rachel grabs her files and slides past Simone's little daughter, who is attempting to tear the head off a sock monkey.

"Oh no sweetie, gentle! Monkey is our dolly baby!" Andrea gasps.

"Our dolly baby? Seriously?" Simone shifts her attention off Peter and onto his sister. "You know, we've been really careful about that. We don't force gender stereotypes on our daughter. And Jamie is naturally curious; she's really pushing against the world right now. It's developmental. Gentle?" Simone snorts. "Jamie is a warrior woman. Jamie will not be oppressed by social *expectations*."

"But," Rachel hears on her way through the office. She can imagine Andrea's hands twisting in her skirts. Andrea has three children with various fathers who are, at best, incidental. The fact that not one of them pays child support is a sure trigger for Simone, even more so than Andrea's present milky maternity.

Joan barely looks up as Rachel passes her desk. "Oh God, are they at it again? Who's winning, Earth Mother or Social

Justice Warrior?" She peers at the paper propped against her keyboard. "Jesus, here we go. No birthdate and a missing postal code. You think one client could fill out a complete form, just one client, one time? My six-year-old could do better than this." Joan has two children, first a boy and then a girl, and neither have appeared at the office except in the school photos flanking a steel cylinder of sharpened pencils. Joan's children are carefully scheduled into ballet and hockey, piano and violin, play dates and calm breaks and earned screen time. A reward chart is tacked to Joan's bulletin board and there are frequent phone calls home. Rachel's heard the one-sided conversations: "I'm taking off one happy point. Right now. No, don't even; it's too late to use your kind words. You blew it, buddy."

Rachel smiles. It's best to humour Joan. "Have a good weekend?"

Joan closes her file and stretches. "Kids barfing with some kind of stomach flu, and hubby in a stinker of a mood. Thank God it was his turn to take them to hockey practice this morning. Family fun, Rache, you must be so glad you opted out. Hey, you try that new café yet? Kinda expensive, but if you don't need to watch your money . . . " She waves at the file Rachel carries. "Oh yeah. Judith wants to see you in her office."

Judith's door is closed. Judith's door is always closed, a managerial technique Rachel suspects is designed to make them knock and wait, to speculate and worry. But Judith smiles when Rachel enters. After an exchange of small talk . . . and Judith is adept at this, knowing to steer clear of children and husbands . . . she lays the file open and pushes it towards Rachel.

"Do you see?" says Judith, tapping the top line with her pen. "Right here. *Describe the nature of your disability.*"

"Yes," says Rachel, "She's filled it out: *Real sick, blood's gone bad. Head heart fingers tose, too bad to get out of bed sometimes and cats complan and are mizerbal.* Spelling doesn't count, does it?"

Judith breathes in then out. "Well, no. But the Ministry needs more information."

"Like what? How many days she's been too sick to feed the cats?" Rachel hears the edge in her tone and so does Judith, whose pen taps a sharp staccato warning.

"Hardly. But this sounds, well, slightly incomplete. She needs a diagnosis that fits our criteria, with names of meds and prescribed dosages. A signed letter from her doctor stating that her symptoms are as described and she's following her treatment plan. The Ministry *hates* it when we send an incomplete claim."

"Goodness, that sounds like a lot of work. Especially for a sick person." Rachel's read the file and can see the woman clearly, as she would a long lost friend. Elderly, alone in a house stinking of damp newspaper and cat pee, the milk souring in the fridge. Cardigan askew and hunched over a cup of tea, past outrage at life's injustices and in a state of perennial confusion, relying on the help only Rachel can offer. An oddly comforting image.

Judith smiles and clasps her hands. "Yes, but not all of our claims are entirely, well, *authentic*. People tend to lack objectivity about their conditions, especially when there's money involved. And you know how the Ministry asks us to be respectful of their budget."

Rachel turns to leave, and Judith waits until she reaches the door.

"Oh, and Rachel? I appreciate that it's not been easy. I really do. I couldn't believe the changeover either, especially at our ages! I have to question Tom's judgement sometimes. But you just let me know if you need anything. If there's anything I can *do*." Judith smiles because there is nothing Judith can do, nothing Judith is required to do, except question Tom's judgement when Tom is not there.

Tom's judgement. Rachel sits at her desk amidst the piles of claims and post-its and thinks about Tom's judgement. Tom's judgement was born of pessimism and doubt, and was therefore almost always correct. Tom's judgment was great. It was his heart that flopped.

Tom was the one who'd pushed the appeal for the Ministry to merge all services into one office. Who'd slammed his fist at municipal meetings, and argued for the convenience of picking up a hunting licence as you paid your land tax, of claiming for disability while you settled your electricity bill. It would save jobs, he'd said, especially in this age of online service. Tom was the one who'd sat behind closed doors with the town councillors and told them the budget cuts were coming and they'd better start pruning. To let him start with the office ladies, some of whom were ancient. Those who were left could take on a few extra jobs at no cost to the department.

And thus, a decade or so before retirement, Rachel was moved from stamping birth and marriage certificates in

Tom's office, from seeing Tom every day and sometimes at night, to processing all the sad cases, the income support and disability claims. It was hard not to take it personally. It was hard not to take it as a warning.

Of course, the others changed jobs too. Joan churned out the licences now, everything from birth and death to fishing, and Andrea handled accident and insurance claims. Judith was promoted from Tom's receptionist to branch manager. But none of these women had been Tom's mistress for years.

Real sick, blood's gone bad. She should at least try to fix this poor woman's claim.

Mistress. Like all antiquated terms, somewhat bloodless and watery in the mouth. What do the young call it now? Booty call? She was Tom's booty call. His good-time girl, his bit on the side.

At one time, he'd thought he might leave his wife. They'd talked in bed over spread magazines. Where they would live and what furniture they'd buy, the dinners they'd cook and the wines they'd cellar. They'd planned a holiday on the Greek islands in a little art hotel where you could sit on the balcony and hear the dolphins sing. Rachel had always wanted to travel, see the ancient cliffs and scrubbed white sand, the sea in gradients of blue. She'd imagined that after they came back, they'd have babies with uncommon names and eye colours, they'd have a sturdy old English pram and the sweetest nursery furniture. Like the pastel things in her magazines, the ones she'd read when Tom wasn't there.

And the other thing. The thing that had happened after that trip. It had been a bad time, the worst, with Tom stressed because his wife had found a lump and his son had punched the principal, and he'd needed her to be something other, something lighter, so she'd seen to it. Before it was even a really a thing.

Head heart fingers tose, mizerbal.

Goodness. She's nicked herself. Something — a staple? — poking into the palm of her hand, bright drops like pomegranate seeds flicking onto the file. Rachel's conscious of the hum of the office then, the busyness: Andrea offering Simone's little daughter a cupcake, and Simone's flat voice intoning no sugar on a weekday, Peter hiccupping laughter, Joan on the phone patiently explaining that no ma'am, you can't arrange the funeral here but it is your legal responsibility to report the death, and for that you need a death certificate.

Strange thing to certify, a death.

Stranger still that she's going to skip from birth to death with no other certification in between. In between-y now, that awkward age. The softness to her waist and upper arms, the crepe feel to her skin, the sudden fevers and wavering confusions. On her last eggs.

Joan's on the phone to one of her kids now — "No . . . no don't you hang up on me or I will text you into next year" — and Andrea is soothing Peter that he is not fat, only a little cushiony. The bell above the door tinkles and a rush of air announces a client. Simone's voice, bright and professional, *good morning can I help you?* Judith strides by and the smell of her perfume is heady and faintly brackish, like flowers left in a vase too long. Rachel wonders if Judith still has sex. What it's like at her age.

Tom hadn't broken up with her. Not exactly. Just a lessening through the years; less often and less time when he did visit, less talk after and no plans at all. Something different in his gaze, a fixed expression around his mouth in the last months. No, he didn't want to discuss it. Everything was fine, just some things happening at home. Of course he would call. When he could. It was difficult. She was not to pressure him. It was the one thing he couldn't stand in a woman.

When he assigned her the new job, he said she should be grateful. Other women her age were getting laid off. Besides, he knew she would be fine. Trooper like her, she could get on with whatever she was given.

Too bad to get out of bed sometimes. Mizerbal.

"Why do you put up with it?" asked Rachel's best friend, twice divorced and merrily single. "Why not come to the city? It's different here; single's *normal*. We'd have a blast, Rache, think of the freedom! You wouldn't have deal with the sanctimonious suburban mommies and their cheat-ass husbands."

But Rachel lives here, in this place, in the same house she'd grown up in and inherited after her mother had passed away. She knows the flex and shift of the seasons, the way the main street has pushed up and branched out like a living thing. She can tell what family a boy belongs to by the set of his ears, and a woman's daughter by the way she rolls her eyes. The suburban mommies are her friends and colleagues. The suburban mommies are Judith and Joan and Andrea and Simone.

It's a kind of symbiosis. The other women imagine a breezy freedom for Rachel: Sunday mornings in the café, weekend getaways and spa retreats, book clubs and art classes and exotic dining. They comment on her small waist and attribute it to unlimited gym time and a lack of pregnancies. They declare envy, then counter it by claiming they would not change a grey hair or single stretch mark, they would change nothing about their child-sprung lives. In return Rachel bakes cupcakes. She sends flowers on birthdays, and starts office kitties for showers and weddings and anniversaries. She listens benignly to the family dramas. She never advises or competes, never contradicts the womanly wisdom thrown around like confetti, and she always admires the accomplishments of other people's children.

And she's thinking about this while she dabs at the blood flecks off the file, on how this is a kind of belonging, a kind of love; she's thinking of the poor woman with the mizerbal cats and how rotten it would be, to be sick and unable to work, how rotten to be old and alone. And even if she sees how they look at her now, the men with vague impatience and the women with a strained benevolence, even so, she's thinking she's lucky, she's lucky to be loved and accepted, when the silence strikes her.

She looks up.

She sees Judith first, palms up and reaching, mouth open to say something to the man in the doorway. He's carrying something long and wrapped in nylon (golf clubs? tennis racquet?) and Rachel sees it's a gun and thinks how silly, he doesn't need to bring his gun to get a hunting license, and then many things happen at once: a high pitched scream, quickly muffled, and Peter frozen, a cupcake halfway to his mouth; Simone, calling *lockdown, Jamie, lockdown!* and her little daughter scuttling underneath the toy table; Judith, her palms opening while the man raises the gun.

"I want . . ." he says.

His eyes are odd: muddy and unfocused. His face has a chalky coarseness to it, like something a child might draw.

"I want . . ." he says again.

"Stay down, Jamie," hisses Simone and the man swings the rifle towards them.

"Please tell us what you want," says Judith.

"I want you to listen."

"We're listening." Judith makes an odd shushing movement with her palms.

The little girl starts to wail, and Simone says *shut up shut up or the bad man* — and the man points the rifle at her. "You shut your goddamn mouth, I'm not going to hurt no kids."

"Please tell us what you want, we're listening." Judith's voice is soft.

"I want you to listen to me. I'm not going to hurt no kids, never would hurt no kids, that's the last thing I wanna do. I got kids."

"You have children? How old?" This is Andrea. Rachel catches the swift look Peter gives her.

"Five. Seven." The rifle swings from Judith to Andrea. Judith's hands sink to her sides.

"Boys or girls?"

"No. You're not listening. I want I WANT . . . " The rifle butt thumps against the floor and someone screams and someone whinnies and someone says *fuckfuckfuck*.

The man thumps the rifle butt again and tells them to shut up. His eyes roll back and then find their focus, muddy as melted chocolate. He's mumbling. Rachel can hear phrases; the bitch, the goddamn bitch, liar liar liar.

"Please tell us how we can help you." Judith is speaking again.

"I want you to listen to me."

"We're listening."

"It's her. See, it's *her*. After they took my job, after they stopped my disability. But see, my head don't stop hurting, hurts all the goddamn time. They put something in there, some kind of damn chip makes me do stuff. But her, she don't listen." The man shakes his head and the motion makes him stagger. "Bitch took my kids. She's poisoning them against me."

"What would you like us to do?"

The man looks at his rifle. He's swaying on his feet now. Rachel wonders if he's drunk and whether this would be a good or bad thing. Maybe he'll pass out. "I want you to call the cops."

Judith barely pauses. "Okay. I can call the cops. Do you want to talk to them?"

"No. Goddamn fuckers. Paid all my child support, regular like, and still got an order. No phone calls no texts no nothing. My goddamn kids. Bitch."

"You want me to talk to them? The cops?"

The man stares at his rifle, wipes a hand across his mouth. Rachel catches a smell, stale sweat, something else. Something tinny and rotten sweet, like a recycling bin left too long in the sun.

"Sir? What do you want me to tell the police?"

The man takes a step forward, sways and catches himself, rocks back on his heels. There's a squelching sound. Rachel looks at his feet. His sneakers are dirty, covered in water or mud and he's left tracks on the floor, rusty tines smudged brighter red in places. *Real sick, blood's gone bad.* Rachel feels her throat close, sees flecks of dark rising.

"Tell them they can stop looking. Tell them I'm here."

Time changes then, becomes porous. Nobody moves for a long moment. Then Rachel is sitting on the floor with the others, her back to the wall and her hands on her knees. They've been herded into Judith's office after? before? Judith calls the police. The room is airless and hot, and stinks of stale breath. Simone has her little girl cradled between her knees and is stroking her forehead and murmuring. Andrea and Peter sit silently together, and Joan stares straight ahead. Judith is the only one not on the floor. She's at her desk, watching the open doorway. The man paces back and forth, his feet squelching and sticking. He's muttering . . . the bitch, she never, never was my *fault* . . . ! and the rifle thumps against the floor for emphasis. He paces and the timber of his voice changes, becomes lower and more rhythmic. When the phone rings they all jump.

"Sir? May I answer that?"

"Answer it. Yeah."

And Judith talks to the police, then the man. "They want you to know that they're outside. They want to know what happens next."

The man paces. "Tell them to wait."

"Do you want to talk to them?"

"No."

The man is standing in the doorway now, the rifle dangling. His mouth moves and his muddy gaze slides around the group. Rachel is aware of holding her breath; she sees Peter flinch and Andrea pull her knees tighter to belly, Simone cover her little girl's eyes. "Tell them they need to *listen*. Then hang up."

The man remains in the doorway after Judith puts down the receiver. His presence alters the room somehow; compresses the space, darkens the light without actually casting a shadow. Rachel tries to breathe without whistling. *Head heart fingers tose, head heart fingers tose.* The man raises the rifle and points it at Judith.

"You. Come with me."

"What?" Judith shrinks into her chair.

"We're going outside."

Judith's feet scrabble and Rachel sees that she's trying to slide under her desk. Her palms raise. "No, no, please — I have three children, a son and two daughters, their names are Mark and Debbie and Pam, and Pam has given me a grandson, his name is Caiden and he's the sweetest — "

"Shut up."

Judith's mouth snaps shut.

The man swings the rifle at Simone, who squeals and wraps herself around her daughter.

"No! You don't hurt kids. You said." This is Andrea. "We're mothers, grandmothers, you can't — you *said*."

The man pauses, then slides the rifle around the group in a slow lazy circle. Rachel feels it pass over her, its cold metal shadow. He stops at Judith. "Choose someone. You have thirty seconds."

"Oh my God," Peter says, "I don't . . . "

Andrea hisses at him to shut up.

Judith stares at the man. "I'm not, I can't . . . "

"Thirty seconds."

The others are looking away; Simone cradling her child, Joan with her eyes closed, Andrea staring at Peter and Peter looking at his hands. But Rachel is watching Judith. Judith's gaze swivels to Rachel, then back to the man.

"Her?" he asks, glancing at Rachel.

Judith's chin dips slightly, then again.

The gun points at Rachel. She rises to her feet. It's effortless, without thought. There's a ringing in her head, and beneath that, some immense thing. The love in this room. She feels the strands of it, how binds these people: fierce Simone to her little girl, Joan to her absent children, Andrea to her unborn baby and to Peter, who sits with his head in his hands. All the mothers and children and partners and friends, the spiralling web, and Judith at the centre charged with keeping balance. Rachel feels the love and how she rips free of it as the man pushes her through the doorway.

The gun presses against her jaw. She feels it digging in like a thorn, and she wants to fall but the man's got her by the scruff of the neck. He's whispering, but maybe that's the ringing in her head, and Rachel thinks how much it sounds like the sea or perhaps the dolphins singing, and she's struck by a terrible shame that this should happen to her, but it's deserved, isn't it? If no one would speak for her? The love of others and the lack of her own, how heavy it weighs! Rachel's knees buckle and the man jerks her upright. They pass through the entry door and the bell tinkles, and a thought crystallises in her head: the opposite of love is not hate, never hate, the opposite of love is expulsion.

The sun hurts her eyes. She lowers her gaze and sees the litter caught in the flower pots, a crumpled beer can and a chip wrapper, the remnant of a plastic bag fluttering like a flag. A discarded nail, rusty and bent. Small things. Then the gun leaves her jaw and her head floats free, she has time to think how absence is felt more keenly than presence before her head explodes and she's on her knees in the dirt, wetness spattering her back and belly and legs and a woman is screaming, screaming until the other voices come and the hands lift her up and shroud her in white blankets.

They give her the rest of the week off work. A week at home because she was not hurt, not really. Rachel wraps up on the sofa and watches television. The story makes the national news, along with a call for greater security in government offices. Much is made of yet another murder-suicide committed by a rejected father. Much is made of the child that was present in the office but not harmed. Judith is interviewed, and denies that her actions were heroic. "Oh, anyone would do the same," she says in her quiet voice. "I'm a mother, a grandmother. You stay calm, you protect the children. It's our *nature*, isn't it?"

Rachel returns to work after the Easter weekend. She brings foil-wrapped eggs, intending to put them out in wicker baskets.

"Rachel?" says Simone. Her face is very white. "We didn't know . . . I mean, we weren't sure if you'd . . . I gave your files to Joan."

The office is quiet and empty. No one comes to her desk and when they pass, they do so with muffled steps and eyes pressing forwards. Snippets of conversation drift by during coffee break. *I knew, a night of bad dreams and I saw my grandmother standing at the foot of the bed, yes, lockdown is something we practise at home because I knew, oh I kept mine home from school that day, called them twice and the sun, something strange about the light so I knew.* Judith appears and calls Andrea. Joan follows her in, then Simone. Peter is nowhere to be seen. The door shuts. Rachel looks for the file on woman with the mizerbal cats, but can't find it. Shortly before lunch, the others leave and Judith asks Rachel to join her.

"Rachel. We all know you've been through a lot," says Judith. "You know, we have some very good people on board. For when there's been a crisis. For when you need *help*."

"But I want to work. I want things back to normal."

"Rachel," Judith clasps her hands and leans forward. "This is not just about *you*. The others, they want to move on. It's hard, well, having you here. You remind them. Simone has nightmares, about what could have happened to her little girl. Andrea's heartbeat was all over the place right after, thank God the baby was fine, but still."

Rachel's head feels hollow, a cave for Judith's voice.

"I talked to Tom. I explained the situation."

The ringing begins in her ears. It's hard to concentrate, to breathe.

Judith reaches into her desk drawer and pulls out an envelope. "He's managed a very generous offer, Rachel. A full pension, a bridging allowance. I think you should take it."

Rachel looks at the envelope. There's a cheque tucked underneath the flap. The sum is huge.

Judith walks her to the door. The office is empty. The sun cuts through the glass and shows the web of lines on Judith's forehead, criss-crossing the corners of her eyes and mouth. "Oh Rachel. I'm so sorry. Can I give you a hug?" Her arms reach out, palms up, and clasp Rachel to her. Rachel smells the brackish perfume.

The robins carol and trill when Rachel walks home for spring is truly here. The lawns are shot with colour, and the first of the buttercups push through the dirt. Something lifts and floats free in Rachel's lungs. I am expelled, she thinks. I am exempt. She breathes in and a scent of rosemary fills her lungs, and she thinks of the Mediterranean, of how the Mediterranean might smell in spring. There's a ringing in her ears, and it sounds like dolphins singing or maybe the sea, the white marble cliffs and the blue blue sea, rolling in and rolling out.

THE THINGS THAT NEVER HAPPEN

1. You die before you are born.

You never sucked air as they dragged you to light, gob-spattered and bloody. There were no photographs of your parents' shocked white faces, of the smiles pasted all round while you raged purple. Your mother never sang *husha husha* through gritted teeth while you screamed your three in the morning arias and your father dreamed of drowning kittens. Neither argued about whose fault you were after lack of sleep had made them brutal.

You are more perfectly remembered as a possibility. Your father trudges through cherry blossoms and imagines a daughter with all the feminine accoutrements: a petal pink blanket, a first pair of toe shoes, a prom dress with rosy skirts. The photographs he'd take and how your exasperation would only make you prettier. Your mother pauses at the department store train sets. You're a pudgy hand pushing cars round the track, you're a rosebud mouth to burr the noise of the engine; oh, you're forever six and sweetened on milk and digestives.

Both parents name you Ariel, after the angel. Privately, and with exquisite sorrow.

2. You are a child brought up in perfect love.

They never shouted. Not when you cut your sister's hair into jagged chunks nor when you shoved a coin up her nose and told her she'll shit gumballs. Your mother didn't swear like a bus stop drunk, when you said you hated her because she wore a frazzled orange sweater to your dance recital. Your father never cried when you stumbled in stinking of cider and cigarettes, your eyes glazed with the gropings of the boy who said he'd love you if you did. And you did.

Your parents sit with you at the breakfast table. The sunlight sparkles off your words and blesses the porcelain, which is unchipped and hued to match the linen. Your mother serves muesli she's made herself, with heart-healthy oats and freshly picked berries, and your father says please when he asks for the milk. They listen and nod and tell you they love you.

We trust you, they say. *We know you'll make the right choices.*

3. You choose to be an artist rather than a customer support officer.

You never ended Thursday drinking with Sharon from accounts, telling her the boss has a fat bum and yes, you very much *would* put that in a memo. Neither did you begin Friday in the boss's office denying all knowledge while you swallowed your sick. And that clinch with Kevin from sales who had bad breath but you'd drunk too much to care? Oh no, that didn't happen, and you wouldn't tell anyone but Sharon if it had.

You work as the spirit moves you. You stalk your London studio wild-eyed, gauze-skirted and braless, you swig from a bottle of absinthe and you never pass out or puke. Oh, how you flame; you hold your brush like a spear and abandon it by dawn light to smear the paint with both hands, so immediate and passionate you are.

The Saatchi courts you and you tell them to shove it up their well-padded posteriors. You're no sell-out.

4. *You meet your true love.*

You never convinced yourself that Kevin's breath was bearable, especially after a few gin and tonics. You certainly never agreed to that post-date coffee in his damp smelling basement suite. You didn't stare over his shoulder at the stain on his ceiling telling yourself this was better than another Saturday night with that cow Sharon, who drank too much and told tales.

You meet your true love in some European city where the rain falls in a silvery Chopin patter against your bare arms. He offers you his umbrella, and holds it cupped over your head while his curls fight the onslaught. *Ah*, he says, *an artiste? D'accord, you go naked in the rain.* His eyes crinkle when he looks at you, and you want to stroke those lines, to feel his corrugations under your fingertips. Later, you do.

You cry at the airport, with your eyes luminescent and your mascara perfectly intact.

He calls you long-distance. He says he loves you too much to lose you.

5. You marry your true love.

You never sat in a dingy bar with your belly rounding under an elastic waistband, telling him you didn't expect anything except the child support payments. He never tore his beer mat to bits and said you might as well get married, you got along all right, didn't you? Mr. and Mrs. Kevin. Awesome excuse for a few days off work and a shindig.

Your true love proposes in a Parisian cafe, his voice curling over the croissants and cream. You bite into a sugar-sweet strawberry, the first one of spring. You make him wait for your answer.

A cathedral or a country house? Fiji or the Bahamas? You fret, and drop a dress size without trying.

Don't worry, he says. *Paint. I'll arrange everything.*

You wear a weightless white dress and your mother something muted, and everyone is elegant and thrilled and sober in the photos.

6. Your youngest child survives.

You never hit an icy patch with one hand on the wheel and the other thwacking your oldest boy, who pestered and poked despite your best threats. You never sat through the *did you* and *did you not* while the police officer took notes and your husband took the children. Time didn't stop when the cot was dismantled and the playsuits bagged for charity.

Your little one bounces when your foot hits the brake, cosseted by the car-seat belt that you have so methodically fastened that morning. You always listen for that safe solid click, no matter your headache or the rain or the *mummy*

mummy mummy. You pull over, and you soothe his shocked cries.

Your baby grows up, three steps behind the others and running to catch them, through summer sand and first snow, through packed lunches and birthdays and sports day heroics. So quick.

You place the track and field trophies on the mantelpiece, next to the oldest child's graduation photo and the middle one's ballet certificates.

7. *You fear the good life's left you complacent and you travel to Nepal.*

You never took your first shot of vodka before the afternoon soaps, with the laundry undone and the cheese growing mould. Your husband never left work on a hunch, never found you sprawled in a puddle of pills and vomit. He didn't stroke your wrists in the cold light of the emergency room and promise that you'll both get through this.

Your children all graduate from university and find promising jobs and pleasant partners. Your youngest comes out as gay and how your friends talk, but what do you care? He's better-looking than their children and your paintings are selling for thousands.

But you find yourself unsatisfied.

You book with a reputable company and spend a tedious month in Kathmandu acclimatising to the altitude while posting witty updates on Facebook. The climb is long and hard, but you make sure to take pictures of the view and the tattered prayer flags, of a bundle of rags the guide says is someone not so fortunate.

You show your photos over spring Beaujolais in the conservatory while your guests flutter and exclaim. *Oh, how changed you must be.* You agree and your husband holds his glass aloft.

To change, he says. *Il est nécessaire.*

8. Your husband leaves you for the intern he's rescued in the rain.

Your husband never held you when you were unwashed and full of hate, when you shrank from your children and wanted nothing but sleep. He didn't bring you the first of the snowdrops and place them on the windowsill when you said their smell hurt your head. He wasn't there when the sun caught the petals and you thought you might live. You never noticed the flawless kindness in his eyes, despite the balding head and terrible sweaters, and you never fell in love with him years after you'd married.

Your true love holds your hand over the smoked pigeon breast in your favourite eatery. He tells you publicly, so you cannot make a scene. You do so anyway, and take a special joy in the Bordeaux two hundred bucks a bottle and dripping from his forehead.

You will paint this later, in stormy grey and bilious yellow. The Saatchi offers six figures and you accept. Divorce is so costly.

9. *You live longer than you could imagine, longer than you could
want.*

You never found perfection once removed, in the children
of your children. You never fed them candy before bedtime
nor let them run wild in the summer night, smirking at your
daughter's protests. Your husband didn't pale and clutch at
his chest while you prayed to the God you never believed
in. He didn't live to tell you the lump you found in your left
breast was probably nothing, but you should get it checked
anyway, and he's not there to help you choose the verses
you'll be remembered by.

You never have time to say thank you for the snowdrops
and the way they catch the light.

You live alone in a magnolia-painted condo. You
lunch with friends, you paint, and you think you might
do Cambodia next year. Your children visit, as polite and
perfect as you've demanded they be, and you wonder if they
ever tore your flesh and grappled at your breast.

Sometimes you sit by the window at five o'clock in the
morning, watching the ashy light extinguish the stars.
There's a whispering in your head too soft to understand:
fragments of an old song, a half-remembered conversation?
You strain to hear and the silence settles in.

Life is very long, you think. Not remembering where the
line has come from, not knowing how to paint it.

HOLD

IT BEGINS WITH THE LAKE. There's that sense of skimming sun-danced surface, my hands slapping and scooping heavy water, my legs churning beneath me. Stop fighting it, they say, and you'll float. I take a deep breath in. My lungs fill like birthday balloons and I let myself fall forward. Hold and float, hold. My limbs lift and drift as weightless as white weeds, and my blood fizzes with oxygen. Hold. The sun seeps in through eyes sealed shut and I believe. I believe as my muscles uncoil and my bones soften. I believe as the happiness bubbles out of my mouth and my head fills with summer. It's true. I can float like this forever. Breathe deep and hold. A disturbance then. My legs feel it first, that tendril of cold uncurling from the blackness beneath, sure as a snake, bringing a shadow with it. It ripples across my belly and winds into my mind. Nothing, it whispers, this lake holds nothing. My eyes snap open. The deep gapes below me, immense and empty, waiting. Equilibrium prickles and totters and I fall awake, breathless, my lungs remembering the dark and my hands clutching for him. Hush now, he'll say with his caramel voice pulling me to surface, and his brown eyes smiling next to mine.

Of course, this does not happen.

A panic attack, they say, a night terror and nothing more. A normal reaction to loss. The body deals with grief even when the mind cannot.

౿

"That lake," they said back in the summer I turned eight, back when I was learning to swim in cold water. "That's a true mountain lake. Deep, you know? The sun only warms the surface, the bottom stays dark as winter. Takes some kind of disturbance, a passing boat or a seasonal wind, and that chill seeps right up. You know you can drown in that current? And the water's so cold you'll stay down forever."

It was true. I remember the accidents every summer. Dread passed through the crowd like a shadow over sun. The lake would empty while the ambulance waited, the driver eyeing up the teenage girls knotted together and shivering in their bikinis despite the heat. A fence of adult legs would ring the casualty and I would be pulled away. Once I saw a white-faced boy spew water, once I saw a covered stretcher. Sometimes nothing but clusters of people stilled and silent, all eyes turned towards the lake.

Sonya had her own version of the lake. She showed me her painting, symmetrical, the fold line dripping with dark. I thought I was looking at a butterfly, with each side a mirror image of the other.

"It looks very beautiful." I did not want to offend. "But you're supposed to use bright colours and you forgot to put on antennae. Butterflies use their antennae to feel where the wind blows." I wanted Sonya to know I was smart for my age.

"You're looking at it the wrong way," she said and turned the paper on its side.

"The lake," she said, "The lake holds another world. Do you see? Down down down." She ran her finger through the wet paint. "You gotta go *down*. You gotta break through the cold, and you'll come up the other side. Guaranteed."

I looked at her painting again. Sky, land, midnight blue water, all done in broad brush strokes. A dark line in the middle and then the same, in reverse. Lake, land, sky. Dark blots danced on both sandy shores, repeating upside down and through the water.

"Then what?" I said. "What's on the other side?"

"The world you want," Sonya told me, "Like here, but better."

I could not disagree. Sonya was nine, a year older than me, and lived in a lakeside trailer. All year, not just for the holidays.

We were renting the double-wide down the road from Sonya that summer. Our trailer had a den and a hot tub. Theirs had peeling panels and curtains drawn tight at all times of the day. "I doubt they have air conditioning," said my mom, "but there's a girl about your age living inside." I was sent with a jar of homemade jam in hand.

"My mom's still sleeping," Sonya said when she answered the door. She cocked a hip against the frame and stared at me. Her cutoffs were too short, and I could see the heart pattern on her underwear where it showed through the holes.

She took the jam from me and popped the lid. A finger rude and wild poked its way into the jar, swirling and lifting a gob of strawberry to her mouth. I gawped at her feet. They were dirty and bare.

"Carl's at the lake. We can look at his stuff," she said. "If you're quiet." She licked her finger and turned her back. I followed her inside.

Her room was dusty dark and smelled stale. She plopped herself on the bed and leaned over the side. Her t-shirt rode up, exposing a knobby spine. She pulled out a cardboard box and undid the flaps.

A record album cover, a man staring bare-chested on the front. His hair tousled cherubic, his arms spread and ending where wings would begin. We stared at this for some time.

"Jim." said Sonya as she slipped record from gauzy cover, "Carl says he's the Truth."

His voice droned and insinuated from the speakers as Sonya pulled things from the box. Each was named and solemnly passed to me. *Rollies*: a tiny red envelope with little square papers inside. I crinkled these between my fingers, and they were as pretty and as ephemeral as butterfly wings. *Joss*: a powdery dark stick that left a sweet residue on my skin. And finally *Miss March*: a grownup lady spread bare naked on glossy paper. Sonya placed her across from the album cover with the angel man on it. The two sets of nipples stared at each other.

The bottom of the box was filled with bottle caps, of all colours and all providences, shining like treasure. Sonya picked up the bluest of these and pressed them into her eye sockets. Blinded, she grinned at me. I chose a gold one, and a silver. Sonya's smile faded behind her blanked out eyes.

"You can't see any more when you're dead," she said, "They put coins on your eyelids to keep them shut."

I clutched at my chest, my eyes rolling and my tongue thrust out. Heart attack, cartoon style. Then I realised that Sonya couldn't see me.

"Pretend we're dead," she was saying, "that we are somewhere else."

Head to head we lay, bottle caps floated on closed eye lids. The corrugated edges dug into my skin but I would not say anything to Sonya. Dead was serious and silent, and needed a sense of ceremony. I tried to think of nothing but I saw my face in the water unafraid, my breath measured and calm.

"My dad's teaching me the dead man's float," I said.

"Carl swims," said Sonya, "He can dive and stay down forever. He knows how to breathe underwater."

We practised holding our breath, that day and the rest. Hold and float, hold. The black dots would dance in front of our eyes like drifting debris. Hold.

We swam on the living room rug, the sofa a far flung island. Sometimes there were sharks, sometimes there were cramps and near drowning. Sonya was competent. She knew the lifeguard hold and the kiss of life, she knew the words to comfort the victim. Hush now you're all right, breathe deep, you're gonna live. Guaranteed.

Sonya's mom stayed in her bedroom at the end of the hall. Sometimes she would emerge blinking in her bathrobe, propelled towards kitchen by the glass in her hand. Sonya and I would stop whatever we were doing to listen. The crank of freezer door shoved open, the crack of tray and clink of ice cube. Then the little pause as if considering, but always the same decision made, always the thud of cupboard door and the bottle upended and sloshed. After this, the slow shuffle back to the bedroom.

"Keep it down, wouldja?" her mother would say as she passed, "You know I work night shift. There's cheese, there's mayo. Make yourselves a sandwich."

Sonya would look at me and mouth the words and I would try not to laugh, my heart twisting a little. The cheese was crusted with green fuzz. We made sandwiches of margarine and sugar instead.

Carl was often at the lake, but sometimes he was around. He was a teenager, which made him like one of us, but better. He was interested in grown-up things. He had a guitar and car, he strummed one and washed the other. He had brown eyes that crinkled when he smoked, he had hair that flopped over his face. We hid in the bushes beside the trailer and we watched him. He sprayed and polished car metal, the sinews of his back muscles rising.

"He has a girlfriend," said Sonya, "They do things, in his bedroom with the door shut."

"We could go into his bedroom. Maybe when he's at the lake?" My belly twisted at the prospect and I felt like I needed to pee.

"No," said Sonya. "We don't go into his bedroom. He'd know."

She threw a pinecone at Carl. It hit the car but he turned anyway, grinning, hose in hand like a lance. He swung his hips to the music playing on the radio, he two-stepped and boogied and the hose came nearer, spewing water. We shrieked and ran. Carl always came close but he would never quite get us.

Caramel Carl. I said his name over and over again when I was sure no one could hear, letting it dissolve like toffee on my tongue. I could smell the smoke from his cigarettes and hear the ripple of his guitar floating above us when we swam the carpet. He looked just like his photo over the fireplace, bare-chested and squinting against the sun, bronze-eyed and golden-haired. Sometimes Carl was around; I could sense him even when he was out of sight. But sometimes he was at the lake.

Sonya and I played Underwater World when Carl was away. We held our breath until the air wavered before us, until we fell backwards onto the sofa. Sonya said that if you did it right, you'd see everything you wanted, you would see heaven. I couldn't ignore the pounding in my head or the bursting in my lungs, I had to draw breath.

"What did you see?" Sonya's face was blotched with red.

I lied. I told Sonya I saw a field full of ponies with long wavy manes.

Sonya would not say what she saw.

That summer drifted on. On weekends, my parents packed the picnic bag and we spent all day at the lake. One such day, I asked to bring Sonya. I thought she would like to swim for real.

My parents exchanged looks over my head.

"I don't think that's a good idea," said my mom.

"Not this time," agreed my father, "you have to realise."

I didn't know what I had to realise, but I didn't ask. I was eight and I knew realising was part of being smart for my age.

The lake was busy on weekends. The sun slapped down, the campfires crackled and wafted their holiday smell of wood smoke. The skinny boys cannonballed off the dock as the pedal boats went by, the swim-capped old ladies did the slow and stately breast stroke. The inner tubes bobbed and drifted in the distance, their passengers lolling shut-eyed and sun-soaked. The teenagers drank stolen beer on the shore, they danced slow and close to their tinny transistor music, and their laughter carried over water. I looked for Carl but could not see him there with the others.

I missed Sonya. But I was learning to survive in cold water.

"The lake will hold you," said my mom. "So long as you let it."

"Why is it called the dead man's float?" I wanted to know.

"Because you just let go. You don't try to swim, to save yourself," said my dad, "You just float as long as you have to. Until you are found."

I let my face fall into the water and the heat and noise faded, the depths opened under me and I was not afraid. Hold and float. I bobbed light as a cork on warm current.

I told Sonya I could float forever and she asked if I'd seen all the way to the bottom.

"The middle of the lake, that's the deepest part," she said, "That's where the teenagers go. You can't see all the way down so you have to imagine it. Below the warm water, below where the fish swim and where the weeds are, and right into the dark. Bottom. Break through that, you'll come out the other side. Carl says they play music all day and all of the night, they dance there and never get tired. Do you see?"

Carl was at the lake. We played his records and we swung our hips, screeching the words. Sonya's mom came out of her bedroom.

"Wouldja gimme a break?" she said, raspy in her bathrobe, "Crappy music, no melody. That guy needs a voice lesson. Right after he gets his hair cut."

Sonya looked at me and I answered back, emboldened.

"It's Jim," I said, "Carl says he's the Truth."

Sonya's mom froze. Her shadowed eyes fixed on me.

"Carl's gone," she said, "He's gone, he's not coming back. Stop this bullshit, you hear me?"

Her breath stank of skin scraped raw and sharp-sting iodine. Her hand rose and I flinched, I could feel the cold water slap of it already. She glared at me and hit Sonya instead.

Sonya sat in her bedroom later, her cheek red. I held my breath and waited for her to speak.

"She thinks he's still under the lake," she said, her eyes steady on mine, "She doesn't know he's here too."

Sonya was gone by the next summer. My parents opened the windows to air out our trailer and told me it was for the best. Both Sonya and her mother needed to get away from the lake.

I could do the front crawl as well as the dead man's float that summer. I could swim to my father far away on his floating tube, I could glide over warm current like there was nothing underneath.

Hold

I was building my own version of the lake by then. The lake was as solid and friendly as a bowl of jelly. It was a summertime pleasure and could do no harm. Then came the hot day in August.

I remember slipping over surface with my hands scooping warm water and my head turning in rhythm. In and out the measured breath, hold and float, hold. A disturbance, a displacement of water, and a cold current wound around my kicking legs.

Then came the impact, sharp and sudden.

The world turned over then and I was flailing. Up turned down, the safety of light appeared and disappeared between my kicking feet. The cold seeped in and the dark spread. I saw a set of hands reaching, impossibly far up and shadowed against a circle of sun, but the more I kicked the further I fell. Then a glow, sensed deep below, and the push of another's hands solid and real beneath me. I swear I heard music as I shot up to the light. I know the guitar chords washed from some place far beneath. I broke the surface and my father grabbed me.

"Damn pedal boats," he said, "There should be a law."

The years passed, the lakeside trailers were replaced with condos and my parents began to take their holidays in Florida. I met my own brown-eyed man. He made my head float and my blood fizz, his voice hushed my fears and his eyes crinkled when he laughed. The brown eyes remained while the rest of him fell away. I held his hands between the treatments, I fed him soup and shakes and swabbed his mouth with water towards the end. I did whatever I could to hold him to me but I could not.

I sleep alone in my marriage bed and I dream of swimming in the lake. The warm surface is an illusion and the dark always looms beneath. I panic. I forget how to breathe and I begin to sink through the layers. I wake with the cold current clutching my belly and my limbs flailing, and I realise that the lake holds nothing.

Sometimes I think I am looking at it the wrong way. I think of the faith needed to float and I hear Sonya telling me to turn it on its side and look again. Do you see? The darkness is only a smudged line between two halves of light, the figures dance perfectly mirrored in this world and the other. Do you see? He's at the lake, he's here too and you can see him perfectly when you need to. Hold. You'll break through the dark, you'll float, guaranteed. Hush now and hold.

Hold.

LOST BOYS

"GWENNIE? YOU WANNA COME OUT? Nice night out here."

I can tell my brother's been crying. There's a thickness to his voice that isn't entirely the beer. I look at Prentiss. He's laid out on the kitchen rug, softly panting, and of no help at all.

"Gwendolyn?"

I nudge the dog with my toe. "Prentiss. Porch, now."

His tail thumps, once, twice. Prentiss was brought home from the animal shelter to take care of my brother, but he won't get up unless there's a good reason. Sloppy drunks and careless crumbs are his bottom line.

"Where's Tom tonight?" I call.

"Dunno. Something about parts, a deadline."

"And the Twinbros?" I can never remember their names.

"Didn't show up."

"Curly?" I'm desperate enough to ask.

"Lying low for a while. Until that thing with the bikers blows over."

Typical. That leaves me. "Prentiss, come. Now. There might be cookies."

Prentiss huffs and rolls onto his feet, follows me out the screen door. I settle into one of the lawn chairs and glance at my brother.

He's staring at the night sky. The moonlight draws out his fine nose and the curve of his cheek, and something snags in my memory. A jar of instant coffee and a triangle punched in a can of evaporated milk, the good mugs out on a tray and the voice of some long ago neighbour prattling to our mother, *Oh what a shame your boy's the pretty one.* Prentiss noses my lap. I palm him a cookie and he settles between us. My brother is perfectly still; no ruffling the dog's head, no stroking the floppy ears. I wonder if he's off his meds again.

"What's wrong, Jimmy?"

My brother snuffles and wipes a hand across his nose, lets out a long breath. "I keep thinking about them, the lost boys. I don't get it. I mean, I get the car accidents, I understand being thrown from a vehicle, landing in a ditch maybe. And a bear eating the remains. I get how that could happen. Or somebody up to no good, foul play, like. But those lost boys? They wouldn't go down without a fight. They'd struggle. There'd be signs of whatever happened, the accident or bear or gang killing. There'd be something left, right? For forensics." He swipes a hand across his face again. "So why don't they tell us? Why don't they *say*?"

"I don't know, Jimmy."

"The thing is, Gwennie, the thing you gotta think about. Lost. The whole idea of lost. What the hell does lost even mean? *Who* is lost? The person who isn't there or the person who hasn't found them?"

"Jimmy, it's late. We got an early start tomorrow, yeah?"

"It's the *wrongness*. They can't be lost. They can't be nowhere. Wherever they are, that's somewhere. And just because you can't see them doesn't make them lost." My brother covers his eyes with his hand. "I can't see you, Gwennie, where did you get to? Are you *lost*, Gwennie?" His voice is weirdly singsong.

"Jimmy, listen. You can stay here for tonight. If you want."

My brother takes his hand from his eyes and looks at it, flexes the fingers. "The thing is, Gwennie? The thing is. What if I got it all wrong? What if it's just that, the not seeing them? The not seeing them that *makes* them lost?"

"Jesus, Jimmy. I don't know. I don't know why it matters. I don't know why you gotta sit on my front porch and drink my beer and talk some bullshit you got off your loser friends."

Now my brother is openly crying. His hands move in tandem, patting up his arms then down again. Prentiss snorts himself awake and waddles off, casting a reproachful look over his shoulder. I feel like a shit.

"Chrissakes, Gwennie, chrissakes," my brother is saying. Pat pat pat. "You're supposed to be helping me."

The thing is. The thing is, Jimmy, I don't know how to anymore.

§

It started with the broken washing machine. Jimmy got it cheap from one of the Twinbro's friends, cash in hand and off the back of a night truck, a real good deal and nothing his little sister need worry about. The thing was, he could fix it up. Fix it up good with some parts from the old one, and the fact that the old one was still working and the new one was not never crossed his mind. Of course, Tom got involved after the boot room flooded. Tom could fix it, Tom could fix anything. To that I could agree; Tom was mighty good with his hands and he *could* fix anything, loved the whole idea in fact. Our place had piled up with things Tom could fix but somehow never did, at least not when we were still together. The washing machine sat in Tom's backyard and Jimmy began showing up in my kitchen, smelling unloved. Of course he could wash his clothes in my machine, just until his own got fixed, like.

It was no big thing to feed him while he was there. I had to cook for myself; I might as well cook for two. And I always liked feeding up a man, especially one as hungry as Jimmy. God knows, Tom never ate much — a nibble here or there then off to whatever new thing he was dismantling.

Tom showed up one night while we were eating. He wanted to tell Jimmy about the washing machine, how he'd figured the problem but didn't have the parts. Of course I offered him a plate and of course he declined. He picked at the salad and broke bits off the bread, standing the whole time and spraying crumbs when he laughed.

We took our plates out to the porch the next time Tom came by. It was no big thing. The nights were on the turn and it was good to sit in early evening light.

Jimmy was around nearly every day by then. I didn't mind. I could check his face for the tell-tale tightness, his hands for that patting thing he did. I could watch for the thousand yard stare and call Dr. Pederson if it all got going again.

That Tom came by so often was a surprise at first. I thought maybe it was me, that maybe he had some ideas that way, and I wasn't sure how I felt about this one way or another. I thought that maybe I could put up with it, having a man around again. And he'd always been good with Jimmy.

It turned out Tom had a motorcycle in his kitchen. In pieces, on newspaper — he wanted me to know that, that he'd put down newspaper to protect the lino from oil and sparks. He wanted me to know he was eating at Mickey D's a lot, and he remembered what I said about salt and fat, and how it was no good for his heart. But it was too damn much trouble to cook, with the motorcycle on the floor and the oven door missing and the part for the microwave still on backorder. And he was real grateful for the food. He'd make me something nice in return, soon as he got on top of the other stuff.

So we took our plates out to the porch on the warmer nights. It was nice, just the three of us and Prentiss. Like we'd done when Tom and I were still married, and Jimmy would come over and join us, before that thing with the crossbow and pigeons. I don't remember much of what we talked about; probably the people we'd known in school, who was getting divorced or fat, who was doing okay and who was going under. If the conversation dried up or got all sad and dangerous, Tom could get Prentiss to roll over and fart on command, and that always made us laugh.

We didn't talk about the lost boys. There was never any weird stuff like that.

I knew my brother was still smoking when Curly showed up with his plastic baggies. Jimmy was supposed to have quit; it interfered with his meds or something. Curly was big and stupid and stunk of Cheezies, and he talked nonstop about The Bitch. The Bitch was his ex, a wife or girlfriend, or maybe a mashup of women, some kind of uber-femme that Curly was dead set against on principle. I made myself scarce when Curly was around. There weren't enough lawn chairs anyway. I did tell him off for the skunky smell drifting through the kitchen window and he took care to exhale into the rhododendrons after that. I could hear the three of them out there, talking about the toxins planted in vaccines and tap water and Coca Cola, and how it was making us all stupid and that's what the government wanted, even if the Bitch said they didn't exactly need toxins to do that. I mean, I could hear Curly talking and Tom saying *yeah maybe could be* and the quick suck of Jimmy inhaling. I don't know when or why the Twinbros starting coming around, but the pair of them leant against the porch posts and agreed to everything Curly said. They always knew someone the exact same thing had happened to, no shit. And it was all part of the plan, the Big Plan they got going to keep guys like them down, out of work and out of luck while the fat cats got the babes and the cars and the big houses in the better part of town. Curly nodded so hard to this that hot ash fell onto his greasy jeans. Tom had to douse the smouldering hole with beer.

But I didn't mind too much. Sure, I had to make some adjustments. I put out Styrofoam and serviettes after someone dropped the third glass from the good set, the ones I got with Canadian Tire money. I gave up on making supper and setting the table, and opened bulk bags of corn chips instead. Curly lit one on fire and it glowed blue. He said that proved it, what he was saying about the toxins.

But the thing was, Jimmy was happy. He sat in his lawn chair and listened, and sometimes laughed with his face all loose and his hands resting on his belly. I guess it was all the talk; Curly skipping from thing to thing, the Twinbros interrupting and running over each other's sentences, Tom reigning it in and steering it somewhere else. All that talk just filled up the porch and left no room for anything else.

The lost boys? That started with something the Twinbros said had happened to a friend of theirs. To their son, a young guy on his way to university which proved he wasn't a dumbass and wouldn't do anything stupid. So he leaves the family home in the morning, says he'll call when he gets there, and he's got all his stuff in the car, his fancy phone and skis and a new bike on the roof rack —

"Asshole," said Curly, "he work for all that stuff?"

"Shut up, he's a good kid," said one of the Twinbros, "and the point is, he's driving alone."

He's driving alone, but he's on the highway. Plenty of people around, right? So the phone rings hours before it should, and the family thinks it's him, he's got car trouble or something. But it's not him, it's the police. They found the car by the side of the road, door wide open and engine still running. Bike and skis still there, i-phone on the console. No sign of the kid. So there's a massive search, dogs and helicopters, even his mom crying on the national news. That was three years ago. Nothing, *nada, zilch.* Kid disappeared without a trace.

"Bullshit," said Curly. "There's always a trace. Bet they covered it up."

"They? Like a government thing?" said Tom. "Why would they do that?"

"Mutated genes, duh," said Curly. "Kid was probably one of those made-in-the-lab kinds, mother's a career bitch and got too old to do it the real way. They can do anything in those labs now; human ears on a mouse, chicken cutlets, a whole baby. Sometimes it goes real wrong. Kid probably starting growing scales or killing sheep every full moon, something like that. G-men want to close that shit down real quick, believe you me."

"So why not just run him over when he's crossing the street? Spike his drink at the next frat party? Why make his disappearance look so weird?"

"I dunno. I'm not a *scientist*." Curly took a long drag on the doobie and passed it to the Twinbros.

"He's not lost," said Jimmy.

"Maybe a bear ate him," said Tom.

"No blood, no guts, no bones. No trace."

"So he sees a bear, stops the car to take a look. The bear grabs him, hauls him away and eats him. Scavengers take the rest and there you are. No trace."

"Why the hell would he get out of the car to look at a bear?"

"I dunno. Maybe he's a *scientist*."

I remembered that Tom could be funny sometimes.

"He's not lost," said Jimmy.

The Twinbros looked pleased with themselves. One of them said, "Bet he shows up three years later, a mile or two from the car and butt-naked in some farmer's field. Not a day older, but burn marks all over his belly."

The talk turned to alien abduction, a hot topic on porch nights. The guys had a fascination with anal probes, which they found both repulsive and hilarious. When they were stoned enough they took turns staring at the stars and swearing they were moving, zooming and zigzagging, disappearing only to show up in another place. One of them would start up . . . "Hey Jimmy they're coming to get you, cover your ass . . . " and the rest would follow with don't drop the soap jokes.

I hovered at the screen door, half in and half out. Funny thing about those nights; the guys didn't talk to me if I pulled a kitchen chair out to the porch, but they seemed to need me around nonetheless.

"Hey, Jimmy, where's your sister?" one of them would say if left.

"Gwennie? Gwendolyn?" My brother's voice.

I didn't mind. The talk was dumb, sure, but the house got quiet sometimes. After Tom left, I used to throw my voice around the place . . . humming, whistling, prattling to Prentiss or the plants . . . just to feel like I was still there. It's true I didn't talk much to the guys, but I insisted that they wipe their feet at the door, broke up the party if I had to work the next day, told them to throw their empties into the recycling before they left. It got so the guys would pause on the doormat like they knew they were supposed to do something, but needed me to tell them what. It was like being married again.

And sometimes it was different. Sometimes, if it was late enough, something real came out. Tom, in tears because he missed his mom, wished he'd phoned her more before she died. Curly telling the others he still bought The Bitch a Christmas present every year, and never got around to sending it. The Twinbros, so hard to tell apart that sometimes they didn't know it themselves, and one would have to call the other just to make sure he answered to the right name. Jimmy, saying he knew his thoughts weren't real but he couldn't stop them; that thinking things through was like trying to do the crossword with a jar of flies let loose in your head.

And that thing about the kid, gone from his car with the engine still running? I thought about it, when I was folding laundry or waiting to answer the phone at work. I remember seeing a movie where the killer dressed like a cop and stopped people on the highway. All of us there in the audience yelled and hooted but they still opened the door, because you would, wouldn't you? You'd think the cop was there to save you. It got to me, that movie. There was something about how the victims were crying, smiling, so damn grateful even as the knife came down, something about everything you trusted gone wrong.

A few weeks passed before the next lost boys story.

It was Curly who told it, and that surprised me. He said he'd read it on the internet. Curly didn't look like someone who went on the internet to read.

It was like the one about the university kid, except this time it was a young man going to see his girlfriend. The driver's door left open, the engine still running. No skis, no bike, no expensive phone, but a can of root beer upended and fizzing onto the seat leather. The police had called an APB and a search.

"They won't find him," said Curly.

"He's not lost," said Jimmy.

The guys went through the usual scenario — government conspiracy, alien abduction — and discounted a bear attack. There would have been teeth marks on the can of root beer. Bears like sweet things. Curly thought maybe it was a beautiful woman, standing on the side of the road in shortie shorts, flagging the kid down. She would have been a blonde with big hair, big boobs, one of them dotty tops that ties in the front and shows off some tanned abs, but not too muscly. Guy would've gunned the gas if he saw all that snaky female bodybuilder stuff going on.

"So how's she gonna wrestle him out of the car, do him in, dispose of the body? Cute little hitchhiker like that?" That was Tom.

"Wasn't her, *duh*," said Curly. "She got the rest of the biker gang hiding in the bushes, just waiting for signal. Gang of bikers could get rid of him easy."

"Why would they want to? Jesus Curly, maybe it don't work for you, but most people need a reason."

"For his organs. They got a cooler filled with ice, they got connections. Rich old codgers pay big money for a new heart or liver."

I leaned in the doorway and listened to them debate how long a human heart could survive on ice. Someone wondered whether the new Harleys had room for a cooler on the back, or whether they'd need a special side car. I wasn't listening;

I was looking at Jimmy. He wasn't saying much, and that wasn't too unusual in itself, but his right hand was patting his left arm. Pat, pat, pat, all the way up and all the way down, switching hands and starting on the other arm. He saw me watching and stopped.

"You know it's all bullshit," I said to him later. "The lost boys? It's just the guys talking. Probably something they heard, some movie they watched and forgot they saw."

"They're not lost," said Jimmy. "They're still here. I gotta believe that."

"Okay, sure. That's probably true." I kept my voice light, my palms open. Dr. Pederson had warned me about arguing with Jimmy too much when he was in one of his moods.

The spring came early that year. Pretty soon Jimmy and I were talking about hauling the barbecue from the basement to the porch, maybe grilling a few sausages for the boys. I can't remember why we didn't. I don't know whether this would have changed things or not.

Tom asked if he could use my printer on the next porch night. His wasn't working after he tinkered with it, trying to find the obsolescence chip that all the new technology has now. The boys brayed and asked him to print out a babe for each of them too; a blonde with big boobs, a brunette with a fat ass. Curly saw me standing there and tucked his chin. "No offence, darling."

"Aw she's fine." That was Tom with a handful of paper. "Gwennie knows what we're like. She don't take offence." He handed me the printout.

It was an article. A real article, from a newspaper I recognised. Some of the words were spelled wrong, but the newspaper's name was there, in big bold letters.

A squad car this time. Engine running, driver's door wide open. The constable had failed to answer his radio and the car was tracked down quickly enough, to a remote road a few miles north of us. His gun was lying on the passenger seat, fully loaded. His dashboard camera was turned off.

"See? I told you it was a biker gang. Not even a cop's gonna mess with a biker gang." Curly was so excited the spit was flying from his mouth.

"He wasn't so young this time." I got that from the last line of the article, where it said he had two teenage children.

"Don't matter. He's a cop, he's in shape. His organs are good."

Tom snorted. "Jesus, Curly. You seen some of those guys? We could put *you* in uniform, stick a badge on you, and you could get yourself some free donuts on your loyalty card."

And the talk passed to a Simpsons episode, the one where Homer's head turns into a donut and he's last seen eating pieces of himself, and the guys agreed that this was the trippiest thing ever. Jimmy didn't join in. His lawn chair was empty.

I found him under the apple tree staring at the sky. "What's up?"

"Why did he turn off his dashboard camera? Why did he do that to us?"

"What are you talking about, Jimmy?"

"We could have *known*. If he'd kept the goddamn camera on, we could have known for sure."

"Jimmy," I could feel my hands rising, reaching for the right words.

"Chrissakes, Gwennie. He isn't lost. You can't be lost if you're still there."

So I agreed, and left him standing there while I went to talk to the guys. I said what Dr. Pederson had told me, about information being sticky and Jimmy's brain being Velcro, about how the weirdest things could snag. I reminded them about the thing with the pigeons and the crossbow, and the trouble after.

"That wasn't his fault. It was dark. You could see how he'd get confused. And he was lucky. He didn't hurt anyone." That was Tom, trying to soften the edges again.

Curly laughed. "He's fine, we're fine. Long as we don't get mistooken for a pigeon, eh?"

But we agreed. Simpsons, babes, baseball and beer: all good. Lost boys, no. No more lost boys on this porch. Lost boys could stick hard for Jimmy.

They stayed for some time, and left laughing at a stupid thing the Twinbros said. Jimmy came inside to say goodbye at the door. There were man hugs, back clapping, arm punches when Curly grabbed Tom's ass. It felt like any other porch night. It felt fine.

But then something changed. The guys didn't come by so often and they didn't stay so long. We had a barbecue. There were sausages and wings and two kinds of pasta salad, but the talk was strained and the eyes kept checking in with me. Tom was the exception; Tom still showed up regularly to sit on the porch and drink beer, to tell us about the new thing he was fixing and complain about the disposable culture, to laugh about who was doing what and who'd got themselves caught. I could leave Tom with Jimmy. I trusted him like that.

It was a porch night like that, maybe late August, early September. I was doing up the dishes and listening to the Tom and Jimmy talk, thinking how their voices were so different from the women at the office: lower, slower, more evenly paced. Comforting.

Then came the crash of glass, a short sharp yelp. Tom's voice, "Chrissakes, Jimmy." He burst through the screen door and grabbed the roll of paper towel off the counter. Prentiss came slinking in behind him, and Tom knelt, dabbing at his paws. The paper towel came away bloody.

Jimmy was gone when I got outside. The porch sparkled with shards of glass, and sheets of crumpled paper were everywhere.

Tom brushed past me. "I'll talk to him, get him home."

"What the hell, Tom?"

He blew out his breath. "Yeah. You know, you should call the doctor. Maybe get him seen again."

I said nothing. Truth was, I was a little pissed. Jimmy was my business and I didn't need to be told.

"Aw, Jesus, Gwendolyn, don't look at me like that. I didn't do nothing. It was him that brought it up. Looks like he's been on the internet, got himself a goddamn collection." He kicked at one of the papers, a printed out page.

"Yeah? You got nothing to do with it, you just sit here and let him talk?" I let my eyes set on him, pointed-like. "You fix your printer yet, Tom?"

"I don't have time for this, Gwendolyn. I need to find Jimmy."

I remembered that Tom could be shifty sometimes.

I read the stories when I was sweeping up. The open door, the engine still running. There were dozens of them, some from place names I didn't recognise. Many were written in broken English and had spelling mistakes, some had bizarre details. A half bitten hamburger, a shih-tzu sleeping in the back seat, a set of clothes strewn all over the road, a voice calling for Michael on a dropped cell phone. There was one from Jimmy's street. Open door, engine running, no trace. No name for the lost boy and the date given was one that hadn't happened yet.

I held that paper and it felt like my head was floating, and I remembered the time Jimmy nailed his shoes to the floor with his feet still in them. He'd missed all his toes except the little one on the left. He told me that the pain was okay, it reminded him of the point.

"And what *is* the point?" I'd asked him.

"I dunno, I saw this thing in a magazine, this ad for old lady face cream," he'd said. "Tissue degeneration and cellular loss, rapid acceleration. The words got into my head and I started feeling them, feeling lighter, feeling my cells drifting from me like ash in the wind. I thought if I held my hand up to the light, I could see through it, so I kept my hand down. See, I knew I was losing substance, floating apart. I knew I was disappearing. I had this crazy idea that the nails would hold me down."

I'd wanted to ask him about the pigeons, why he did it, if it was something like that.

But I didn't. I guess I didn't want to know that bad.

When Tom returned with Jimmy in tow, I gave him the lost boys articles in a black garbage bag and told them both to go home.

I phoned Dr. Pederson the next morning.

❦

Jimmy has stopped crying. He sits perfectly still, so quiet I can hear the distant hum of a night plane somewhere above us. No moonlight now; the clouds must have come in.

"Tell me what to do. Just say it, Jimmy."

It's so long before he says something that I don't think he's going to.

"I keep seeing those lost boys. Standing there, the engine running, the driver's door wide open. Yelling, waving their arms at all the passing cars. No one stopping for them. No one seeing them. It's the not seeing, yeah? By the time the cops come, there's nothing left. There's nobody there."

"What do you want me to do, Jimmy?"

The dark settles between us. I can hear Jimmy shift in his chair, take in a breath.

"Talk to me. Tell me about this, about where we are right now. Tell me everything you can see in front of you."

So I tell him about the airplane, how it's probably on a flight path to Hawaii, Honolulu, Tokyo maybe. I tell him about the rhododendrons that are white but look almost red in this light, and how they never smell of much. I tell him about the apple tree and how, if you stand underneath it and look up, you can still see the frayed rope from the tire we swung on as kids. I begin to describe the lawn, green and clean seeing how Prentiss only uses the neighbour's yard for his dumps.

"Jesus, Jimmy. We should go in. I'm talking about nothing."

Jimmy's voice in the dark. "Can you see me?"

"Of course I can." I squint at his shadowy shape, searching my memory. "You're wearing your blue shirt, the one with funny collar, and your hair needs cutting. I can see you. You're right here next to me."

"It was green. My shirt. But blue's good, I like blue."

Funny thing is I can see the shirt, the green one he's talking about it, I can see it clearly in my mind. I can see him wearing it earlier and slopping ketchup on the front and dabbing it off with a serviette. Pat pat pat. I squint at him again. The shirt looks blue now. "Jesus, Jimmy. Can we go in now? We got an early start tomorrow."

"Keep talking."

So I talk until Jimmy's head nods and bumps a notch, until my voice frays. The sounds and syllables slip into the night, weighting down the dark, shaping it into something. I talk and my brother sits beside me, unseen and unheard, but he's there, he really is, because who the hell else would I be talking to? On a dark night like this?